Unforeseen Danger
A Detective Liv DeMarco Thriller

G.K. Parks

Copyright © 2019 G.K. Parks

A Modus Operandi imprint

ISBN: 1942710186
ISBN-13: 978-1-942710-18-9

For my Aunt Kathy, the greatest aunt in the world.

Thank you for always encouraging and supporting me and everything I do.

ONE

"Idiot." He blew into his closed fist. "What did I tell you?"

"It'll be okay." Keith squeezed his eyes shut. "She didn't get far. I found her."

A million thoughts went through the man's brain. They were almost caught because of Keith, the incompetent moron that he was.

"I can fix this," Keith insisted.

The man glanced behind him. His wife had just finished washing the dishes. Without the water running, he couldn't risk being overheard. She didn't know about his side business, and he had to keep it that way. Silently, he left his office and went out the front door, pulling it closed behind him. "That's right. You are going to fix this. You're going to fix it right now."

Keith didn't like his boss's tone. "Sure. I'll just take her back and put her with the others."

"No. She escaped once. What makes you think she won't do it again?"

"Umm." Keith's insides clenched. He knew he was in trouble. He just didn't realize how much trouble. "She'll behave. I'll take her to the house and tie her up. I'll lock her in her room. Whatever. She won't cause any more problems. You have my word."

"You're right. She won't." The man waved at his neighbor and went to his car. "There's only one way to fix this. Do you understand?"

"But she didn't get far. She didn't talk to anyone. No one knows. It's fine. No harm done. It'd be a waste to get rid of her."

"Bullshit. Have you seen the news reports lately? The police are on to you. To your activities. How long do you think it'll take them to connect you to me? I can't have that."

"My activities?"

"Yes, your activities. You promised me no one would miss them. That you were careful and methodical. But you were wrong, just like you're wrong now. The police are investigating. They know women are being taken. They don't know why. They're already asking questions. What if someone noticed her? Can you guarantee she didn't speak to anyone?"

Keith glanced over at the frightened girl. She was barely old enough to be considered a woman, and he regretted every decision he made that led him to this point. "Does she even speak English?"

Frustrated, he let out another sigh. "It's time I clean house. I never should have trusted you with this. I didn't have these problems until you came along."

"But, sir, you don't understand. This is not my fault."

"No. You don't understand." The man gripped the steering wheel tightly. He'd been running this operation for years and never encountered a problem, but the moment he brought on this new guy, everything went to hell. If he didn't cut ties, he'd get caught. And he couldn't afford that. He had built an amazing life for himself. He couldn't let one idiot sabotage everything. "Kill her and don't leave a mess."

Keith cursed. "Yeah, all right."

"Make sure it can't be traced back to me."

"Don't worry, boss. I got this."

"I doubt it." The man stared out the windshield at the manicured lawn, the flower garden, and his expensive house. He never would have been able to afford any of that on his salary, and Keith's mistake could cost him everything. His wife. His wealth. And his perfect life. "You remember how I took care of you, paid your debts, got those dealers off your back, and made sure your son's treatments were covered?"

"Yeah, and I appreciate that."

"Circumstances have changed."

"C'mon, man. I told you I'd take care of it."

"You caused it. Now fix it."

*   *   *

"Heads-up, Liv. We got movement," Detective Brad Fennel, my partner, said.

"Copy." I leaned against the brick wall. After a few ineffectual clicks from the empty Zippo, I tossed the lighter into my bag and rummaged around for a spare. The cigarette dangled from my lips.

The man walked right past me. I didn't look up, but I felt his eyes travel the length of my body. He didn't slow or stop. When he was a safe distance away, I turned to watch him jog up the steps of a nearby apartment building.

"False alarm," Brad said in my ear.

"No kidding." I gave up the search for the nonexistent lighter, tucked the limp cigarette behind my non-radioed ear, and glanced around. "How long have we been out here?"

"A little over five hours. Are you all right? Do you need a break?"

"I'm fine, just tired, bored, and a little cold."

"You should have gone with regular nylons. Fishnets don't provide much warmth."

"Speaking from experience?"

He chuckled. "Just observation. One has large holes. The other doesn't. It's science. Kind of like how you need butane to get the lighter to work."

"You know I don't smoke, and no matter how bored I get, that's not going to change." I ducked my head down to hide the grin. "Besides, Emma would kill you if I took up smoking."

"Why would that be my fault?"

"I don't know. You're my partner. You're supposed to have my back. She would see it as a failure on your part." An evil thought crossed my mind. "She'd hang your balls from her rearview mirror. It'd serve you right."

"How's that?" Brad asked, clearly confused.

"You do realize I can hear you sipping your coffee and crunching on something. Those better not be the chocolate chip cookies my mom made."

"You're hungry. Why don't you grab something from the mini-mart?"

"Processed oils and refined sugar, are you insane?"

"Fine, I'll save you a few cookies, but your mom made them for me. And I must say, I would have never known they're grain-free. They're delicious."

"Bastard."

Brad laughed, a deep, velvety sound that immediately improved my mood.

We returned to radio silence. In the last several weeks, four women had gone missing. The first two were working girls. It wasn't odd for transients and people on the fringe to disappear or move on. Missing persons and vice explained the first two disappearances away easily enough, but the next two were a little harder to discount.

The third woman reported missing, Lyla James, was a twenty-year-old theater major. She lived in the dorms, worked as a waitress, and performed in some community plays whenever she got the chance. After Lyla missed one too many classes, campus security knocked on her door. Her belongings remained, and they found her car in the parking lot. The only thing they didn't find was her.

Missing persons began a search. But since Ms. James didn't have a dormmate or family, by the time the police were notified, she'd already been missing for more than a week. The police spoke to her classmates, coworkers, and friends, but no one recalled exactly when they saw Lyla last. It had been too long.

She'd been raised in foster care. Her foster parents hadn't spoken to her in months, and her classmates thought Lyla's disappearance was just Lyla being Lyla. I didn't know exactly what that meant, but apparently the woman liked to unplug from the word for weeks at a time. At the moment, the detective in charge of her case was still holding out hope Lyla would return.

When another disappearance occurred, Captain Grayson insisted the intelligence unit would investigate. The fourth victim, Abigail Booker, was last seen getting into a blue sedan with a man only a few feet from where I stood. Like the other missing women, Booker was also in her early twenties. She'd dropped out of school and worked odd jobs to make ends meet. Like the others, she didn't have any significant ties, but we'd gotten lucky with Booker.

She always met her friend, Nicky, for coffee in the morning, and when she didn't show, we'd gotten the call.

The missing women didn't exactly fit a profile. They were all thin and pretty, but that's where the similarities ended. They had different eye and hair color. They weren't even the same ethnicity. Normally, offenders liked to find victims with the same characteristics, so I didn't think we were dealing with a serial killer or rapist. Truthfully, we weren't even sure the cases were connected. Missing persons received reports of new disappearances every day, but based on the reports, the two prostitutes worked this neighborhood and Lyla James had been performing in a play a block from here and worked at a nearby restaurant. If these women were abducted, it had to have happened here. This location was the only discernible connection we'd found, so that's why Fennel and I were camped out on the street.

"Someone's approaching," I said, giving the tall, blond-haired man a seductive smile. He quickly diverted his eyes and hurried past me. "Never mind."

"He didn't fit the profile," Fennel reminded me.

"I doubt we have an accurate profile."

"Well, according to Nicky, Abigail Booker had just started seeing some guy before her disappearance. Trim with dark hair and glasses, and Lyla's coworkers remember seeing a man who fit that description at the restaurant a few times. So it could be something."

"Or nothing." I looked down, making sure my badge was hidden inside my open blouse. It wouldn't help our surveillance to broadcast I was a cop. Maybe I looked too much like a whore or not whorish enough. Or we were barking up the wrong tree.

If they were taken against their will, then the abductor didn't have a type. But I was more than half a decade past his victim's age range. The makeup and poor lighting would help with that, but since we had next to nothing in terms of leads, I couldn't help but feel this was a waste of our time. There had to be a better way to find these women. I just didn't know what it was.

Another hour passed. I strolled up and down the block, watching the passersby. It was almost four a.m. But this area was just a stone's throw away from several clubs, theaters, bars, and restaurants, so foot traffic remained consistent. I ducked into a twenty-four hour mini-mart and purchased a large glass bottle of sparkling mineral water. Wrapping it in a brown paper bag, I stepped out of the store, unscrewed the top, and took a sip.

"Last call," Fennel said. "Keep your eyes peeled."

Since the bars closed a few minutes ago, there was a fifteen minute window where the streets became crowded with taxis, rideshares, and the occasional drunk driver who didn't live within walking distance. The sidewalks were another story, full of people stumbling around, pissing in alleys, and vomiting in bushes. Sometimes, it was hard not to find the human race disgusting.

I took a seat on a step just outside an apartment building and held the wrapped bottle between my knees. As I glugged down some water, I kept my head on a swivel. Two men nearly got into a literal pissing match on the corner, and a woman and her date got into an argument ten feet from where I sat. She slapped him, and he grabbed her wrist and yanked her into his chest.

"Liv, don't," Fennel warned. "Let it play out." My partner knew how badly I wanted to intervene, but domestic issues were always messy and rarely resulted in anything positive.

After a few angry whispers, he released her, and the two went up the steps to the apartment building. "Freaking skank. We should call the cops," the man muttered as he pushed past me.

"Asshole," I retorted, but the door had already slammed shut.

Taking my bottle, I moved off the steps and found a spot at the side of the building, barely within visual range of Fennel's unmarked car. I capped my bottle and looked around. As predicted, the streets had nearly emptied. The quiet seemed so much louder now, almost foreboding.

"We'll give it another thirty minutes, and then I'm calling it," I said.

"Roger."

Ten minutes later, a car pulled to a stop at the far end of the street. With the headlights shining in my eyes, I couldn't determine the make or model. After thirty seconds, a man stepped out, and the car drove away. As it went past, I noticed it was a red, late model sedan. Nothing special. Probably just another guy looking to make a quick buck schlepping people back and forth.

I leaned against the corner of the building. From this distance, I couldn't make out much about the guy, but since no one else was around, he had my undivided attention. He wore a dark hoodie. One of his hands was in the front pocket, and the other carried a bottle-shaped brown paper sack, just like mine. Except I didn't think he was concealing mineral water.

A familiar squawk sounded in my ear, but the message was staticky and garbled since I was hearing it secondhand through our open comms. However, Fennel's voice came through loud and clear. "Dispatch just got a report of a disturbance. It sounds like a domestic."

"Where?" I asked, suspecting I knew the answer.

"The apartment building right behind you. Unit 34C. Patrol's on the way. What do you want to do?"

I turned and headed up the steps. A car door slammed behind me, and Brad jogged across the street. While I waited for the elevator, Fennel entered the apartment building. This wasn't a ritzy place. There was no doorman or front desk. The front door didn't even have a lock.

The doors dinged open, and the asshole from earlier stepped out of the elevator. He kept his face down and pushed past without even seeing us. Brad gave me a look.

"Go check on the woman," I said, watching the front door swing closed behind the man.

"No. I'll go after him. You check on her."

"I can't like this." I gestured at my clothing. "It's probably a false alarm, anyway. Go upstairs. I'll meet you at the car. Radio if you need assistance."

"I left the radio in the car."

"Then call my phone." I didn't give Brad time to protest before I ran for the door.

The asshole stormed down the street, and I slowed, doing my best to keep him in my sights without tipping him off that he was being followed. Once Brad gave the all clear, I'd stop pursuit, but in case this prick had roughed up his girlfriend, it'd be easier to make an arrest if we didn't have to search the city to find him.

He stopped on the corner, kicked an empty can across the street, and banged his fist against the Plexiglas shelter surrounding a bus bench. After a few minutes of working off his aggression, he sat down and leaned forward, scrolling through the numbers on his phone. He sent a text. Then he dialed a number.

"Hey, man, I know it's late, but can you do me a favor? I'm gonna need a place to stay." He waited. "Yeah, she did. You said she would." He paused again. "Great. Just one more thing. Do you think you could pick me up?"

My phone buzzed, and I fished it out of my purse. "Yeah?"

"She's upset but otherwise unharmed. Patrol just got here." I turned to see the blue and white parked in front of the building. "I'm going to update them and get the details straight. It doesn't look like she wants to press charges, so I'll be down in a minute."

"Okay." I pressed the disconnect.

The man at the bus stop was oblivious to my presence, too wrapped up in his own drama to be aware of anything else. I kept my distance and slunk away, glad that I'd glued felt tips to my heels to keep them from making too much noise on the quiet street. Despite everything, my cover remained intact. I should have been thrilled. Instead, I was annoyed.

I'd only gone a few steps before movement in my periphery caught my attention. The man in the dark hoodie was pacing back and forth in an alley. He smashed the bottle he carried into the brick and circled again, putting both hands on his head and tugging at his hair. He wiped his sweaty palms on his pants and rubbed his face. Seeing me, he completely stopped like a deer caught in headlights.

Nonchalantly, I leaned against the wall, removed the cigarette from behind my ear, and went in search of the Zippo. I repeated the same routine as before, but my presence spooked the man. He left the alleyway and went into the nearest building. I found his behavior disconcerting. He appeared to be in the midst of a crisis. And before I thought about what I was doing, I followed him inside.

TWO

He had a decent lead, but since the elevator was waiting in the lobby, I knew he took the stairs. He was several flights above me. His angry, unintelligible mumbles echoed against the hard, flat surfaces. He stopped on the landing of the twentieth floor and jerked the door open, but he didn't enter.

"Dammit." He let the door go. "I can't. I just...fuck. I gotta." His voice cracked, and he slammed his palm against the door. "I gotta." He sniffed. "I gotta."

The emotion and resolution in his voice made my insides quiver. "Excuse me, sir," I called.

He glanced down the steps. "I'm busy, lady. Go home." Pulling the door open, he disappeared from view.

I ran up the steps as fast as my legs could carry me. Call it cop instinct or woman's intuition, but I knew he was about to do something terrible. I just didn't know what it was.

I burst onto the twentieth floor. He was at the far end, waiting for the elevator. Racing down the hallway, I reached the elevator just as the doors closed. He disappeared behind the solid metal. I tapped the call button repeatedly, but the elevator was already ascending. I read the flickering display at the side. When the numbers continued to climb, I ran back to the stairwell and up the steps.

By the time I made it to the top floor, I could barely breathe. Forcing deep breaths into my lungs, I dialed Brad and left the line open. With the phone tucked in the front pocket of my bag, I stepped onto the roof.

The man didn't turn at the sound of the door opening or my ragged gasps. His sweatshirt clung to his back, and he stared off into the distance. He stepped onto the ledge, and I was suddenly afraid spooking him might cause him to fall.

At the academy, we were taught what to do in these types of situations, but the biggest takeaway was to keep the person calm and wait for help to arrive. The department had professional negotiators and crisis management teams to deal with jumpers, but if I didn't do something soon, he was going to die.

He took another step forward. His toe caught on the edge, but, somehow, he managed to regain his balance before tumbling thirty-eight stories to the ground below. He let out an uneasy chuckle, the perspiration stains growing on the back of his sweatshirt.

The sound of my muffled footsteps caught his attention, and he looked behind him. "Mind your business, lady. I told you to go home. Why are you following me? Are you lost or something?"

"I don't live around here."

He chuckled. "Great. You can get out of here before it's too late. Go."

My heel caught, and I tripped. I scraped my knee and tore my stockings. Thankfully, the glass bottle inside my bag didn't break, and everything else remained intact.

He glanced back at me. "Jesus. You're a pro."

"It's better than being an amateur." I brushed myself off and got to my feet. "I could probably show you a trick or two. What do you say? It's a nice night, and it's not like anyone will bother us up here. I'll even give you a discount."

"I'm not really in the mood. In case you haven't noticed, I have other things on my mind."

"You don't want to do that."

"Maybe I don't, but it's not like I have a choice. I gotta do it." He was serious. I just wasn't sure what prompted his insane decision.

"Why?" My internal voice cringed. Asking why wasn't recommended. Clearly, the man was distraught; asking could lead to an impetuous and irrevocable act.

"Get the fuck out of here." He turned around, reached into his pocket, and threw a fistful of cash at me. "That's what you want, isn't it? Just take it and go. Get out of this neighborhood. And stay out."

His eyes were red. His face splotchy. It was obvious he'd been drinking, but what caught my attention was the outline of the gun beneath his sweatshirt and the red flecks covering his front.

In a split second, I decided to stick with my hooker persona instead of announcing I was a cop. I didn't need him to pull his gun. Cop-assisted suicide wasn't on the menu, but I'd be forced to draw on him if he presented as a threat.

I whistled. "For that much cash, are you sure you don't want to go out with a bang?"

He laughed, a sick, maniacal sound that twisted my stomach into knots. "I already have." He turned away from me, balancing on the ledge. He held his arms out and walked back and forth as if on a tightrope. "You know, when I woke up today, I had no idea it'd be my last. I guess that's how it goes. You never know until it's too late. You're just going about your business, and you get a phone call. It's always a fucking phone call, isn't it?"

"Who called?"

"He did."

"He?"

He looked at me, confused why we were having this conversation. "Why are you asking me questions? Did he send you?" Agitated, he tugged the gun free from his waistband. "He fucking sent you, didn't he?" He waved the gun around, not quite aiming. "Answer me."

The brownish-red specks covering his clothing could only mean one thing, especially paired with the forty-five in his hand. He shot someone at close range, and now he was contemplating offing himself and probably me too.

My hand slipped inside my bag, and I palmed my gun. "No one sent me. Do you want to tell me what happened? I've been told I'm a great listener."

Something caught his attention, and his eyes narrowed. He waved the gun at my chest, teetering on the edge and nearly losing his balance. "What's that?" He jerked his chin at my exposed bra.

"They're called tits. Jugs. Hooters. Whatever you prefer."

"No." He pointed more emphatically with the weapon. "That."

I knew better than to look down, so I kept my eyes on him. The run up the steps exposed my badge. This suicide attempt might just turn into a homicide. Well, another homicide, from the looks of it. He pulled back the hammer and set his jaw.

"Seriously, dude," I held up one palm, "you don't want to do this." I had to think fast, especially with the way he was waving the gun around like a sparkler on the Fourth of July. "Shooting me would be a big mistake."

He rubbed his face with the back of his gun hand. "Yeah, I know. But I didn't have a choice. And I don't have one now."

"Sure, you do." It was time to announce.

"No, bitch, I don't. I gave you a chance, but you just ran up here like some damn hero. Who the hell are you? Did he send you to finish the job? That bastard didn't believe I'd have the stones to go through with it. Son of a bitch."

"No one sent me." I tugged on the chain around my neck. "But if you tell me what's going on, I promise I'll help you. I'm Detective DeMarco. I'm with the police. And trust me when I say the last thing you want to do is shoot a cop."

He didn't exactly believe me, but he couldn't make the facts fit with what he was seeing. Based on the glazed look in his eyes, he was high. He might have thought this was just a bad trip because he broke out into a fit of laughter, practically doubling over as he held his stomach. "Un-fucking-believable." He could barely speak since he was laughing so hard.

I edged closer, hoping to grab his gun. He wiped his eyes with the back of his hand, still waving the forty-five around like it was a toy. I reached for the muzzle, but he jerked away from me and aimed. "I won't have any of that. What's in the bag? You got a gun? Let me see it."

"Yeah, fine." I shrugged and moved closer. "I got some smokes and a bottle of hooch too, if you want."

"What kind of cop are you?"

"The kind that needs the occasional pick-me-up."

"Yeah, okay." He eyed the brown paper bag. "That sounds good."

I handed him the bottle and dug through my purse, apparently oblivious to the possibility of any real danger. He tucked the gun into his waistband to unscrew the top. As he took a sip, I removed the handcuffs from my bag.

"What am I supposed to do with this?" He peeled off the bag and tossed the bottle of water to the street below.

I grabbed his forearm and yanked, pulling him off the ledge. He tumbled to the ground, and I cuffed one of his wrists. Realizing what was happening, he jerked his other hand away from me and went for his gun. I kneed him hard in the kidneys, leaving a patch of blood from my skinned knee on the back of his shirt. CSU would not be happy about that.

He bucked, knocking me off of him like a rodeo bronco. He fired blindly in my direction. The bullets went high and wide, impacting nowhere near me. The gun clicked empty. Obviously, he never bothered to reload before coming up to the roof.

By now, Fennel had found us. He burst onto the scene, gun aimed, commanding tone to his voice. "Police. Freeze. Hands in the air."

The man dropped the forty-five with a clunk. He looked at me, a desperate plea in his eyes. "You can't help me. No one can."

"On the ground." Brad moved closer. He kept his gun aimed on the man, who rocked back and forth on his heels. Sirens sounded below us. "I called it in. Additional units are on the way." Fennel came up beside me, and I clicked the second bracelet around the man's other wrist. "Are you okay, Liv?"

"Fine."

Fennel turned him around and pushed him against

the ledge. "Do you have any sharp objects in your pockets? Knives, needles, anything that may stick me?"

"No." The man took a ragged breath. "You can't do this. You can't. I gotta do it. I don't have a choice. You don't understand. Just let me go."

"We'll keep you safe," I promised, watching him tremble and shake.

Brad finished patting him down and hooked a hand around his elbow. "Come on, buddy. We'll get this sorted. You're gonna be okay."

The officers who responded to the domestic were the first ones on the roof. The man looked past me, the fear leaving his eyes. In that moment, I knew. I felt it.

The jumper inched backward. "He'll find me. I don't have a choice." He stared into my eyes and jerked out of Brad's grip. Immediately, he threw himself backward over the ledge.

"No." I ran forward, reaching for him.

Fennel nearly got a hold of the man's ankle, but the jumper slipped out of his grasp. The man landed on the sidewalk, his legs at an odd angle. I stared down at him, frozen by the horror, my brain unable to comprehend what just happened. But my training took over, and I forced air into my lungs.

"Fuck." Brad turned away. He told the officers to call it in and secure the scene.

"He shot someone." I licked my lips. "He's covered in blood, and it's not his. We have to find his victim. He or she might still be alive."

THREE

"Whoa. Where do you think you're going, DeMarco?" Officer Roberts said with a level of condescension that made my blood boil. "I didn't realize they reassigned you to suicide watch. Do you want to take him in? I'll let you keep the collar." He snickered. "ME should be here in a couple of minutes to scoop him off the sidewalk. I heard you already cuffed him. Excellent police work. Real topnotch."

"Screw you." I took a step back and let the other patrolman rope off the scene. I pointed to the discarded weapon. "He isn't just a jumper. He shot someone before coming up here. Maybe you should notify homicide."

"Oh, so now he's a killer too?" Roberts asked skeptically.

"I don't know, but whatever happened made him want to off himself."

Roberts gave me a look. "Did you follow him from some other crime scene? I didn't see your car outside."

"Very astute. It might be because I was conducting

surveillance and happened upon this."

"In that case, this is probably the most action you've seen in a while." Roberts held out the radio. "I'll let you call in your suspicions. This is your mess, Olive. You can clean it up."

"It's Liv," I hissed. "Contain the scene. No one in or out."

By the time I made it to the street, someone had covered the body with a sheet. I felt lightheaded and sick, and as more police cars arrived, I felt even worse. Fennel instructed several units to canvass the area. My partner had the man's ID and wallet in an evidence bag. Keith Richardson, thirty years old, 5'10, 165 pounds, brown hair, brown eyes. A patrol unit was on the way to his apartment.

Fennel and I exchanged a look. We hadn't spoken since the roof. We'd been separated. It was protocol for an officer involved death.

Brad's brow furrowed. *Are you okay?* he mouthed.

Before I could say anything, two unmarked cruisers pulled to a stop at the tape line. Captain Grayson stepped out of one car, and two men with detective's shields got out of the other. Based on their attire, they were internal affairs. Regular cops never stayed that crisp and fresh. We always got a little dirty.

"DeMarco," Grayson waved me over, "are you all right?"

I watched the two IA investigators approach Fennel and shake hands. "I'm fine, sir."

"You know how this goes. Keep your mouth shut, DeMarco. You're entitled to have your union rep present. We'll get this sorted. Until then, I can't have you out here working."

"We didn't do anything wrong, sir."

"I'm sure you didn't. It's just policy." He glanced over at the body. "Unfortunately, he's in cuffs. IA will want to know what happened."

"They're my cuffs." Ignoring the warning look, I continued. "We don't have time for this. That man shot someone before going up to the roof. He was terrified. He was convinced someone was going to get him. We pulled him off the ledge and cuffed him, but he freaked. He broke loose and dove over the side. There's nothing we could have done." I took an uneasy breath; the final look in the jumper's eyes was burned into my brain. "We have to find his victim. I saw him get dropped off maybe thirty minutes ago." I described the red car, Richardson's demeanor, and everything he said.

"All right." Grayson grabbed his radio. "I'll keep it in-house. Our unit will handle it. I'll notify hospitals to be on the lookout, and we'll pull nearby footage and see what we get on that car. I'll have area patrols on alert. Do we have his address?"

"Fennel pulled it from his ID and sent a patrol unit to check it out."

"Do you and your partner have your stories straight?" he practically whispered.

"Nothing to get straight."

"Good."

"Sir, this is my case." After what just happened, I'd never let it go. I had to know what provoked Keith Richardson to jump to his death.

"We'll see. First, you have to be cleared. You're probably looking at twenty-four to forty-eight hours, depending. But I'll see what I can do to get it expedited."

"Detective DeMarco?"

I spun around.

"Alan Pierce, internal affairs division." He scrunched his face together in thought. "Rough night?"

"I've had better."

"Yeah, me too." He eyed my appearance. "Let's take a ride. I'm sure you probably want to get cleaned up and change out of those clothes." He eyed my bag. "Did you discharge your weapon?"

"No, sir."

Pierce nodded. "Mind if we test you for GSR, anyway?"

I resisted the urge to say something sarcastic. If my father had taught me anything, it was not to mouth off to IA. I went along with what the investigator wanted, knowing it would only get worse once we were back at the station.

Detective Pierce led the way back to the sedan, and I caught a brief glimpse of the other IA detective getting behind the wheel of Fennel's car. Brad was smart. He'd be fine. He didn't do anything wrong. But maybe I did.

As we drove back to the precinct, I couldn't help but think of every tiny decision I made that led to this point. I didn't wait for backup. I failed to announce, and I didn't maintain a hold on the cuffed man. But no matter how I looked at the situation, one thing was clear. No matter what Fennel or I did, Keith Richardson would still be dead. Nothing we could have done would have changed that fact. The man was determined to take his own life. Even if we had managed to bring him in, we'd probably find Richardson hanging in his cell or worse.

"DeMarco," Pierce said, tapping a beat on the steering wheel, "any relation to Captain Vince DeMarco?"

"He's my dad."

"How's he liking retirement? What's he up to these days?"

I conducted enough interrogations to recognize the

tactic. Pierce wanted to create a rapport. He wanted me to believe he was just a friendly guy I could trust.

"He's keeping busy. He has a new puppy to train."

"What kind of dog? Don't tell me he got another German shepherd."

"Bernese mountain dog."

"He'll be huge."

"Probably." I gave Pierce a sideways look, letting him know I was on to him.

He pretended to ignore the look and went back to tapping a beat on the steering wheel. When we arrived at the precinct, he parked near the back door. "Go get changed, and bandage that knee. I'll meet you upstairs."

"Yes, sir."

The next few hours dragged on. I answered questions, explained the situation, why I was alone, how I came to be on the roof, and handed over my service weapon for inspection. The patrolmen who attempted to assist in the apprehension of Keith Richardson wore bodycams, just like most uniformed officers. More than likely, Richardson's last few moments were caught on camera. It'd be easy enough for IA to pass judgment, but as usual, there was red-tape and additional factors to consider.

When Pierce had everything he needed, I went back to my desk to type my report. Brad was at his desk, but we didn't speak. We knew better. We didn't have anything to hide. We didn't do anything wrong, but IA made even the cleanest cops feel dirty. Fennel finished his report and went to speak to the captain. By the time I looked up again, Brad was gone. Until the verdict came back, we were off duty.

After turning in the paperwork, I grabbed my bag and drove home. Home these days was the spare room in my best friend's apartment. Emma didn't mind having me around, or so she said. With all my long-term undercover assignments, I had given up my place, and with work being what it was, I never had much of a chance to look for something new. Maybe that's what I'd do today. It's not like I'd be able to sleep. Every time I closed my eyes, I saw Richardson's body smash against the asphalt.

As I went down the hall to Emma's apartment, I noticed the man leaning against the door. "Hey," I said, digging for my key, "why didn't you knock? Emma would have let you in."

"I didn't want to bother her," Fennel said. "I couldn't remember if she was working days or nights. I thought she might be asleep." He stared at me with those soulful brown eyes. "But we need to talk."

"You know we're not supposed to. If IA has more questions, they'll have to bring us both in again and any other cops we've spoken to."

"Like I give a shit."

I snorted. "Afraid I threw you under the bus?"

"No."

I contorted my face in mock horror. "Did you throw me under the bus?"

"Liv, this is serious."

"I know." I pushed the door open. Remembering Brad's history, I said, "It isn't your fault. I've thought about it, and there's nothing you could have done differently. Richardson was determined to end it all. He was hesitant at first. I thought I could reason with him. I tried. God, I tried." Deflating, I sunk onto one of the stools at the kitchen counter.

"I heard." Brad opened the fridge and pulled out half the items in the crisper. He grabbed a frying pan, poured some oil into it, and placed it on the stove to heat. "He could have killed you. What were you thinking? You call me and leave an open line, but you don't bother to tell me exactly where you are. Until he threw the bottle off the roof, I had no idea where you were." He angrily chopped the vegetables. "You shouldn't have been there. I told you to check on the woman in the apartment. Instead, you ran off after some asshole. You didn't know if he was armed. What the hell were you going to do?"

"The same as you. And that guy wasn't the problem. Richardson was." I glared. "Since when did you become so sexist?"

"I'm not."

Emma stepped out of her bedroom, dressed in leggings and a tank top. Her rolled up yoga mat hung from her shoulder, but from the look on her face, I wouldn't be surprised if she decided to wield it like a club. "Bradley," she said, her voice an icy warning, "do you want to tell me what's going on in here?" She eyed me, cocking her head at the sight of my shield still hooked to my belt. "Is this your lunch break or something?"

"No." Brad stared at me. "Why don't you tell her what you did tonight, Liv?"

I maintained eye contact with him, even as he continued to chop the veggies. Maybe he'd lose a finger. It would serve him right. "Damn. You did throw me under the bus."

"Liv," Emma tugged on my arm to get my attention, "talk to me. What's wrong?"

I ignored her. My focus sharp on my partner. "What did you tell IA?"

"Nothing, Liv. I didn't tell them anything. Just what happened. You know I would never do something like that to you. But you owe me an explanation. What the hell were you thinking going after that guy alone? And on the roof?" He slammed the knife down. His breath catching. He spun around, leaned against the sink, and stared out the window. "Richardson shot at you. He could have killed you. And you didn't even have your gun out. I want to know why."

"Whoa," Emma dropped her yoga mat on the floor and sat on the stool beside me, "someone needs to tell me exactly what's going on." She looked me over from head to toe. "Are you okay, Liv?"

"I'm fine."

"But someone shot at you," she said.

"Richardson discharged his weapon. He wasn't aiming at me. I made a judgment call. If I had pulled my gun, he would have aimed. He wanted to die, and I wasn't going to be the one to pull the trigger." My voice cracked, and I bit the inside of my cheek. "It's bad enough he jumped off the roof after I handcuffed him. You heard our conversation. You know how scared he was."

Brad nodded. "Yeah."

"Yeah," I said. Emma squeezed my hand, and I squeezed back. "I don't think I'm going to make it to hot yoga today, Em. But you should get going. You don't want to be late."

"Are you sure?"

"I'm sure." I did my best to give her an encouraging smile.

Brad turned to the pan, checked to see if the oil was hot enough, and added the vegetables. He pulled some leftover steak from the fridge.

"Are you chipping in for groceries this week?" Emma asked.

Fennel reached into his pocket and slapped a few bills on the counter in front of her. "Next time, get the crimini mushrooms. The ones you bought suck." They exchanged a heated look I didn't entirely understand, and Brad nodded. "I'll take care of this."

"You better." She gave me a hug, whispering to call if I needed anything, and left us alone in her apartment.

When breakfast was ready, Brad divided it up onto two plates and put one in front of me. He grabbed two forks and took a seat beside me. "This looks great, but I'm not hungry." I pushed away from the counter. "I'm actually kind of queasy." He looked down at his plate. "I know, but you should eat a few bites. The rest will keep until later." He chewed slowly. Clearly, I wasn't the only one who didn't have an appetite. "I can't lose you, Liv. I can't watch more of my teammates die. I just can't."

FOUR

"Honey, is that your phone?" his wife asked. She rolled over in bed and looked at the clock. "Who could be calling this early?"

"It's work." He'd been awake most of the night, worrying something had gone wrong. And of course, it did. "Go back to sleep." He grabbed the phone and went into his home office, closing the door behind him. *Dammit, Keith. Now what did you fuck up?* He let out a sigh and stared out the window.

The phone rang again, and he answered.

"Sir, I'm sorry to bother you."

"It's all right. What's going on?" he asked.

"I take it you haven't seen the news."

"Assume I haven't." He'd been playing this game long enough to never let on that he knew anything. As far as his colleagues were concerned, he was clueless. They might have even thought he was incompetent or just playing politics.

"Right, well, the police responded to a suicide a few hours ago. A man jumped off the roof. He had a gun."

"So? A good percentage of Americans own guns."

"Yes, sir. But he was covered in blood. Someone else's blood. The detective of record believes he killed a woman before offing himself. The police are searching the city for his victim. The media has picked up the story. CSU is processing everything. It's a mess. I just wanted you to be prepared. I didn't want you to get bombarded when you arrive."

"Thanks for the heads-up. I'll see you later."

"Do you need me to revise your schedule?"

"No need. It's just business as usual." He hung up the phone, barely able to keep the calm, cordial indifference to his tone.

This was bad. Keith was supposed to take care of this. What was the point of leveraging someone when he couldn't even complete a simple task? He never should have let Keith become involved in his operation. Keith stumbled upon it by accident. The idiot had heard whispers and observed a few things he shouldn't have seen. But that's why he'd paid Keith to look the other way. And it worked, just a little too well.

Keith had never seen that kind of money in his life. And he wanted more. To get more, Keith provided a list of women, young, pretty, and unattached. No one would miss them. No one would even notice. That's what Keith promised. And for a while, that was true.

Now everything was crashing down around him. And he had to stop it. That's why he told Keith to fix this. The bastard was supposed to get rid of the flight risk and off himself someplace quiet and unassuming. Keith wasn't supposed to make a spectacle and draw the attention of the entire police force.

"Shit." He slammed his palm down. The cops would be all over this. They wouldn't stop until they found Ingrid. He hoped Keith properly disposed of her body.

Without a corpse, there was no crime scene. No evidence. No crime. It was just speculation. And he could live with that.

But something told him Keith left him with an even bigger mess to clean up.

*   *   *

"Who the hell is this guy?" I asked. For the last several hours, Fennel and I had scoured the internet for information on Keith Richardson. We found several in the city, but none of them matched our jumper. "Are you sure that's the right address?"

"That's what his driver's license said." Brad tried another search, but it proved just as useless as everything else we tried. "I wonder what they found at his apartment."

"We're not going to know until we're cleared. Dammit." I squeezed the bridge of my nose and circled the living room. Dropping onto the couch, I closed my eyes. "Why isn't this working?"

"We're not thinking clearly." Fennel yawned and closed the lid on my laptop. "I should take off and let you get some sleep."

"No, not until we figure this out." I checked my phone, but I didn't have any messages. "Richardson shot someone last night. I know he did."

"It's too late for us to do anything about it."

Brad took a seat beside me and reached for the remote. He flipped to the twelve o'clock news. There was a brief mention of a suicide from the roof of an apartment building, but no mention of the victim's name or anything related to additional crimes.

"Police are still investigating," the reporter concluded.

When the weather came on, Brad changed the

channel. He put on cartoons, removed his off-duty piece from his hip, put it on the coffee table, and stretched out his legs. "Do you remember sick days as a kid? Y'know, staying home from school, watching cartoons all day, and eating chicken soup?" He glanced at me. "Grayson's on top of this. Detectives Loyola and Sullivan will probably cover for us, and they're good police. They know what to do. So let's take a sick day. Cartoons and whatever's in the fridge. What do you say?"

"It's not a sick day. We're basically suspended."

"Shh." He closed his eyes. "We're pretending."

"Are you five?"

"Sure, that works." He raised one eyelid and looked at me. "What else do you have to do today?"

He was right. I'd exhausted all avenues of investigating, and my usual means were barred until IA concluded its investigation. I hated being in this predicament. "What about the abductions?"

"Guess Sullivan will have to buy some nylons. I bet he's smart enough to get the regular ones instead of fishnets."

I chuckled at the thought of hard-nosed Arthur Sullivan in drag. That thought, along with the TV, kept my mind entertained until the commercial. I opened my mouth to say something but noticed Brad had fallen asleep. We'd been up all night. The stress and long hours had finally taken their toll. As quietly as possible, I climbed off the couch and turned off the TV.

Brad was right. There wasn't much we could do. The rest of the cops we worked with would handle it. We all swore the same oath, and I had no reason to think they wouldn't uphold it. After a quick change, I settled into bed. Emma wouldn't be home until after midnight, so Brad could stay on the couch as long as he wanted.

After fighting my way through a few nightmares, I woke to a ringing telephone. I reached for my cell phone, but it wasn't mine. Rubbing my eyes, I went to the doorway.

"Yeah, okay. Thanks." Brad hung up the phone.

"How long have you been awake?" I asked.

"Not long. I was just about to take off."

I jerked my chin at the phone. "Who was that?"

"Captain Grayson. He called to tell me to get my ass back to the precinct. He pressured IA to put a rush on it, so I've been cleared."

"It's not like we had any doubts." But there was something he wasn't telling me. "What is it?"

"They found the second crime scene." He sighed. "You were right."

"I wish I wasn't." I glanced at my phone, wondering when Grayson was going to tell me to come in and assist. "Homicide?"

"Uh-huh."

"Did we get an ID on the vic?"

"I don't know. I'll find out when I get there."

"I guess I should get ready."

"Grayson said IA's still checking on a few things." Brad watched my face fall. "Maybe you should call your dad. He might be able to get the ball rolling. I don't want to see you jammed up over this."

"I'm not going to have Vince DeMarco pull strings on my behalf. That's exactly why half the department thinks I made detective. I refuse to prove them right. I can do this on my own."

"All right. Let me see what I can find out. I'll call if there's something you need to know." He snorted. "So much for a sick day."

After Brad left, I ate breakfast, even though it was late in the afternoon, and went for a run to clear my head. My phone rang, and I answered, out of breath. It was Dad. By the time I got back to the apartment, Vince DeMarco was waiting inside for me.

"Jesus," I lowered my gun and clutched my chest, "you know better than to break and enter."

My dad held up the spare key Emma had given my parents. "I have a key, but nice try."

"What are you doing here? I told you I was fine. Did Fennel call? I told him I could take care of this myself."

"Your partner didn't call. My old partner did."

"Captain Grayson?"

"He told me what happened. Are you okay, honey? You should have called me."

"It's fine. I'm fine. IA's just doing their job. I'm sure I'll be back to work soon."

"Did you contact your union rep? I can make a few calls. I know a couple of guys down there. They can recommend a good lawyer."

"I don't need a lawyer."

"Okay, but you know it's my job to worry. Have you eaten dinner yet?"

I shook my head. "Now you sound like Mom."

"Ooh, low blow," he teased, "but, under the circumstances, I'm taking you out to eat. We can talk. Not talk. Whatever you want."

"You don't have to do that. I'm okay. I'm just waiting to go back to work."

"Seriously, honey, you'll be doing me a favor. Your mom left me to fend for myself tonight, so she can paint a pot or something." He rolled his eyes. "I don't get it."

I tried to explain the appeal of painting coffee cups and other ceramic knickknacks while drinking wine and chatting with friends, but the concept was lost on my dad. Frankly, it was a little lost on me too. Emma would have been able to explain it better. After all, she's the one who introduced my mom to the concept in the first place.

Giving up, I showered and changed and let Dad take me to my favorite restaurant. Maybe Brad had the right idea and a sick day was just what I needed.

FIVE

"Who is she?" I flipped through the crime scene photographs, stopping on a close-up of her face.

"We don't know. She didn't have an ID. Her prints aren't in the system. ME's checking dental records, but they haven't found a match yet. Based on liver temp, she's been dead for a little over a day." Brad leaned closer. "She was killed during our estimated window, a few hours before Richardson took the plunge. I'm not sure how homicide felt about us taking over their crime scene, but it's one less on their plate. So they should thank us."

"Forty-five?" I pointed to the three bullet holes in her chest.

"Yeah." Brad rocked back in his chair. "Same caliber as the gun Richardson had. CSU pulled the casings off the roof. Same type we found near her body." He flipped through the papers and pointed to an evidence photo. "Ballistics should be back any minute, but I'm guessing this is the woman Keith Richardson murdered."

The coroner estimated she was between eighteen and twenty-five. Young, blonde, and pretty. "Anyone report her missing?" It had been a day and a half since the incident on the roof. By now, someone should wonder where she was.

"Not yet. I asked my buddy in missing persons to keep his ear to the ground. He'll let me know."

"What's Jane Doe's connection to Keith Richardson?"

"I don't know yet. We've hit a snag. It appears our jumper isn't who he claimed to be."

"I noticed."

I leafed through Richardson's file. The address listed on his driver's license was bogus. The house belonged to a married couple, who according to property records had lived there for thirty-five years. Officers questioned them, but the couple never sublet or took in tenants. They didn't have any children, and they didn't recognize Richardson. Their neighbors were questioned, but no one remembered seeing Keith around. He didn't have a birth certificate, at least not one we could find. Brad spent all morning on the phone with the social security office. Simply put, our jumper didn't exist. His prints weren't in the system, which meant he didn't have a record.

"Identity theft?" I speculated, but that theory didn't hold water. An actual Keith Richardson would have to exist with our dead man's credentials for this to count as identity theft.

"It doesn't look like it. He didn't have any credit cards on him."

"You found the cash on the roof." I anchored my foot on a metal rung and swiveled back and forth, replaying every single thing Richardson said to me. He never told me his name. He never told me much of anything, except that someone made him do it. "Why did you jump? What were you so afraid of?"

Unfortunately, the copy of his license couldn't answer my questions, and neither could Fennel. Rubbing my palms together, I climbed out of my chair. "I'm missing something, and I can't see it. Want to take a drive and check out the second crime scene?"

Brad grabbed his jacket and followed me down the steps. Even though I only missed one full shift and part of another, I was a million miles behind. This is why I hated sick days as a kid. Sure, it might have been fun to stay home and play hooky, but having to make up the homework and assignments sucked. And it still did.

In my absence, uniforms had run down the red sedan. It belonged to Wallace Lee, a rideshare driver. He picked up Richardson half a block from where Jane Doe's body was discovered. That was actually how we happened upon the crime scene. Richardson's phone probably could have shed some light on his actual identity and his associates, but it was practically obliterated in the fall. I didn't know if the techs would be able to salvage enough of it for it to be of any use. Nothing was ever simple.

If Brad and I hadn't been staking out that particular neighborhood, we might have missed Richardson's arrival and never discovered the jumper's connection to the dead woman. She'd probably just end up another unsolved murder. On the bright side, at least we knew who killed her. We just didn't know why.

"Do you think they're connected?" I glanced at my partner.

"Richardson and Doe? Yeah, of course."

"No. The four abductions. The women. Jane Doe fits our profile. Young, thin, pretty."

"Every woman under twenty-five basically fits our

profile. Am I missing something?"

"Richardson wanted to be dropped off in that specific neighborhood. He chose that building for a reason. Do you really think it was a coincidence we just happened to be there?"

"Dumb luck," Brad suggested, but he didn't believe it.

"Did anyone in the building recognize our jumper?"

"The canvass didn't turn up much of anything. We got a few maybes but nothing solid."

A thought flitted across my brain. "He told me to go home, and when I said I didn't live around there, he said that was a good thing."

"The guy was off his rocker." But from the corner of my eye, I could see Brad flip through the photos. "Do you think he shot Jane Doe and caught a ride home?"

"I don't know. If you were going to kill yourself, where would you do it?" My mind went to dark places, remembering the day I found Brad unconscious in his living room. He said it was a mistake. He just needed an escape and had way too much to drink, but ever since that day, I worried about him, probably more than I should.

He mulled the question over. "I don't know. I've never thought about it. What about you?"

"Most suicides do it somewhere they're likely to be found. At home, the office, somewhere with meaning."

"Do you think he lived in the building?"

"Possibly. He knew exactly where to go and did a decent job avoiding me. I'd bet my paycheck he's been inside the building before."

"I have a hunch. After we're done here, let's swing by the restaurant where Lyla James works, and we should talk to Abigail Booker's friend again too."

Realizing what Brad was thinking, I could practically kick myself for not having thought of it first. "Trim, dark hair. You think Richardson abducted those women. But where are his glasses?"

"Maybe he has contacts." He reached for his phone, hitting one of the programmed speed dials. "I'll ask the coroner to check."

"I'm surprised we didn't get the official report yet." Only the preliminary evaluation had crossed my desk. They hadn't even begun the autopsy, not that we really needed one. I was no doctor, but I knew damn well what killed Richardson. "Have you seen the toxicology screening?"

"No, but I'd say he was on something besides the booze." Brad held up a finger to keep me quiet while he asked one of the assistants about the contact lenses. She promised she'd have the coroner check, and someone would get back to us soon. "Thanks, Carrie." He smiled and hung up.

"Carrie, huh?" I shook my head and chuckled. "Are you still seeing her?"

"From time to time. Why?"

"No reason, but I don't want this to end badly for us."

"Us? Explain that to me, Liv. How is this an us? Are we having a threesome I didn't know about?"

"In a manner of speaking. Y'see, she gets serious. You don't. Or vice versa. Someone gets her heart broken, and the next time we need a favor or a rush on a victim, we're stuck waiting for days, weeks, months," I glanced at him, "years. So you do the screwing, and I get screwed over."

"You're being ridiculous."

"It happens."

Brad let out an unhappy grumble. "Don't worry about it. We're not serious. We're not exclusive. We're not really anything." I opened my mouth to say something, and he shot me a sharp look. "And she knows it. Actually, she insisted on it. We're just blowing off steam. She calls the shots. I'm just along for the ride. It's no big deal."

"You better be careful, Fennel. You're gonna get a reputation."

"Is that why you're keeping ADA Winters at arms' length?"

"Among other reasons." I should have realized this conversation would take an ugly turn. Squinting at the street signs, I found a parking space on the end. "Oh, look. We're here." Spotting remnants of the crime scene tape, I opened my car door and took a deep breath. I had no idea what to expect, but from Fennel's rigid posture, I automatically assumed the worst.

CSU had processed the scene. Everything had been swabbed and printed. The killer didn't bother to conceal the crime or his involvement. He didn't care if he was caught. He probably figured by the time we discovered her body he'd already be dead. And he was.

"We wouldn't have found her if we weren't looking," Brad said. "I just wish we knew why this happened."

"Me too." Actually, I was surprised Captain Grayson was allowing us to investigate. The killer was dead. The case was closed.

"She was behind there." He jerked his chin at a shredded and stained mattress. "He probably found it near the dumpster and used it to conceal the body. Patrols actually thought a homeless person was using it as shelter since it was propped at an angle against the wall."

"I bet that officer was quite surprised." I knelt down, searching beneath the dumpster. "Did they check the trash?"

"Yep."

I brushed my hands on my pants and straightened. "Jane Doe didn't look homeless. She didn't have a wallet or ID on her, but she had a gold bracelet, right?"

Brad nodded.

"So it probably wasn't a mugging, not that we found any indication on Richardson's person to think he was a mugger."

"He had plenty of cash though, so maybe we shouldn't rule it out completely." Fennel and I often took turns playing devil's advocate to keep our theories from becoming too insular. But in this instance, I didn't appreciate it.

"Why kill her?" I spun around the tiny alcove. Several trash bins lined both sides of the triangular opening.

"That'd be easier to answer if we had any idea who either of them was." Fennel put on a rubber glove and examined the mattress. The hole ripped in the middle had a clean edge, probably from a knife. His eyebrows knit together.

"What is it?"

He removed the label. "This came from the Monthly Stay Condos. See the name."

"Is there a room number?"

"No."

"I doubt Richardson carried the mattress out just to hide the body. It was probably already here, but it won't hurt to check." I was baffled. "What else is around here? I don't see any clubs, restaurants, or trendy stores. So why was a young woman hanging out in this neighborhood at night?" The area wasn't known for drug or gang activity. Actually, it wasn't really known for anything. It was commercial, offices mostly. Everything shut down by dinnertime.

"Let's find out." Brad took off the latex glove,

tossed it in the dumpster, and marched up the steps to the closest office building. He smiled at the receptionist and flashed his badge. "Detectives Fennel and DeMarco. I just need a moment of your time, ma'am."

The gray-haired woman at the counter looked up with an automatic smile. "What can I do for you?"

"Have you ever seen this woman before?" He showed her the photo on his phone.

"She's pretty. She might be with Rogers and Stein on the fourth floor."

"Rogers and Stein?" I asked. "Is that a law firm?"

The woman laughed. "Goodness, no. It's a modeling agency. Women come and go all the time. I'm not sure about that one, but she looks like she could be a model. Don't you agree?"

"What other offices are in this building?" Fennel asked.

"I'll get you a copy of the directory." She rummaged through a few drawers before finding an old, creased sheet of paper. After struggling to get out of her chair, she waddled over to the copy machine. It was ancient, older than the crap we had at the precinct. After several minutes, it finally warmed up, scanned the page, and printed a duplicate. When she handed it to Brad, it was still hot. "Is there anything else I can help you with?"

"The fourth floor?" I asked.

"Yes," she eyed me, "but you should know Rogers and Stein is closed today and tomorrow. They're remodeling." She laughed, finding it funny.

Brad looked at me, but we didn't know enough yet to ask any other questions or break down doors. I shook my head, and Brad thanked her for her help. He read the directory. Fifteen offices. And this was just one of many nearby office buildings.

"I'll give Mac a call and ask her to get started building corporate profiles."

"Have her start with the modeling agency. That's probably our best bet."

"Still, at that time of night, the office would have been closed."

Fennel shrugged. "It can't hurt to check."

SIX

Our next stop was the Monthly Stay Condos. Despite the fancy name, it had all the makings of a no-tell motel. While Brad spoke to the desk clerk, I wandered around, glancing in windows and any open doors. It was the middle of the day, but half the parking lot was full. And from the noises coming from 502, it sounded like someone was having quite the party.

Spotting a few vending machines clustered together, I stopped in front of them. I could hear voices coming from inside the closest room, but I couldn't make out what they were saying. It sounded like two women, and at least one of them was crying. Under the circumstances, I knocked on the door.

"Hi," I offered a sympathetic smile to the tall, black-haired woman, "I was wondering if you had change for a five. The vending machines only take dollar bills."

She sniffed and wiped her eyes on the back of her hand. "No, sorry." She moved to shut the door, and I inched my foot forward to prevent her from doing that.

"I don't mean to intrude, but is everything okay?"

"Da."

Russian, maybe. I detected a slight accent but couldn't quite place it. My gaze swept what little I could see of the room. Two other young women sat on the bed, watching TV. She stared down at my foot, bumping the door against it to encourage me to move.

"Sorry to bother you."

She nodded, and as soon as I removed my foot, she slammed the door in my face.

"Liv," Brad called from across the parking lot, "are you ready?"

Filing the oddity away for now, I returned to the car. "What did the desk clerk say?"

"He didn't recognize Jane Doe or Keith Richardson. I tried to get a look at the guest registry, but he won't turn it over without a warrant. And let's be honest, this appears to be a cash-only kind of place."

"They probably take credit cards too. They just aren't required. Anything on the mattress?"

"He says the last tenant trashed one of the rooms. Slashed the bed. They had to replace it. And instead of having someone haul it off, he tossed it in the nearby dumpster."

"Did you ticket him?"

Fennel grinned. "I threatened to if he didn't tell me who rented the room."

"Nice."

"I guess. I got a name and a copy of his driver's license. Randolph Sawyer. He doesn't look anything like our killer, but we can still follow up." He reached for the radio and called it in. A minute later, we got Sawyer's current location. He had been arrested for drug dealing.

"I bet I know why he slashed the mattress," I

quipped.

"I bet you're right." For a moment, Brad took in our surroundings. "Nothing indicates Jane Doe or Keith Richardson was here, but it's only a couple of blocks from our crime scene. And Keith had plenty of cash on him. Maybe he needed it to pay rent. We should probably question Sawyer. We have him for dealing, so if he saw something, we can probably incentivize him to cooperate."

"That's a lot of ifs for a case that's basically closed. Is it worth it?"

Fennel nearly rolled his eyes. "That bastard killed someone and endangered your life and our careers. I want to know why." After I started the car, he added, "And I think there's a strong possibility Richardson's connected to the four abductions."

"All right. To the restaurant." I pointed a finger at the windshield as if leading a charge and drove away from the motel.

The restaurant staff had been questioned at least twice before, but third time's the charm. While Fennel spoke to management, I showed Keith Richardson's driver's license photo to the waitstaff.

"I dunno. A lot of guys look like that. It's hard to tell."

"What about you?" I asked, turning the photo to the hostess. "Did this guy ever eat here?"

She took it, her chin crinkling as she chewed on her bottom lip. "I think he used to be a regular. Ricky something." She scratched her ear and looked to the waitress for help. "Didn't he always request to sit at that table?" She pointed to a two-seater at the end of the row.

"I guess." The waitress shrugged. "I don't know. I never work this section."

"Who does?" I asked.

"Bethany and Lyla," the hostess said, looking at the legend scrawled in crayon at the side of her seating chart.

"I need to speak to Bethany."

"She's out back, taking a smoke break," the waitress said.

"All right, thanks." I went out the front door and wandered around the building until I found someone wearing a white shirt and black apron. "Bethany?" I held up my badge. "I just need a moment of your time."

She immediately dropped the joint and covered it with her foot. "What's this about?"

"Lyla James."

"Did you find her?" Bethany asked.

"Not yet. We're following up on a possible lead." I held out the photo. "Have you seen this man?"

She took the photo and analyzed every inch of the guy's face. She blew a frustrated breath out her nose. "I can't be sure." She handed back the photo and looked up at me. "Do you think he did something to Lyla?"

"I don't know. Do you remember anyone special in Lyla's life? A boyfriend? Girlfriend? Someone she would have confided in?"

Bethany shook her head. "Lyla's eccentric. That's what my mom would call it. She's loud and outgoing. She'll talk to anyone. But it's like she's always on, y'know, like acting. No one really knows her very well. Despite all her friendliness, she actually keeps to herself."

Since Lyla grew up in the system, it might have been a defense mechanism. From the horror stories I'd heard, foster care could be rough. Sometimes, it was a godsend, and other times, a nightmare. She'd bounced around. She must have learned early on the only person she could rely on was herself. That's why no one reported her missing. She didn't depend or trust anyone enough to let them get close enough to miss her.

I handed Bethany my card. "In the event you remember something, even if it's insignificant, give me a call."

Bethany stared at the card for a moment before putting it in the front pocket of her apron. "Some of the others were talking. They said they overheard the cops saying Lyla's not the only woman missing. What's going on? Is it safe to be here?"

"I can't really discuss the case, but as far as we know, this place is just as safe as everywhere else. But it doesn't hurt to buddy up. Don't walk to your car alone. Let people know where you're going and when you'll be back. Just take precautions and be smart. And keep your eyes open. If someone seems off, call it in. We'll be happy to check it out."

She nodded. "Thanks, Detective."

I gave her a reassuring smile. "Thank you."

The restaurant turned out to be a bust, but since missing persons already had the security footage from the week prior to Lyla's disappearance, we requested they rewatch the tapes in the hopes they'd spot our jumper. Our next stop was an advertising agency where Nicky, Abigail Booker's friend, was temping.

She greeted us when we entered, told one of the regular secretaries she needed to use the bathroom, and led us into the hallway. "Sorry," she apologized, "I just started this gig, and they want to keep me around for two weeks. I don't want to give them any reason to change their minds."

"No problem," Fennel said. "We just need a minute of your time." He held out the photo.

Nicky stared at it for a moment. "That's him. That's

the guy Abby started seeing before she vanished. Did this bastard do something to her?"

"You're sure it's the same guy?" I asked.

"Yeah. He drove that blue four-door I told you about."

"Did you ever speak to him?" Fennel asked. "Did you get a name? Anything?"

"No. Abby didn't tell me much. Just that she bumped into him at one of her jobs, and he asked her out. They met for lunch, and they went out maybe one or two more times. I just remember he offered to pick her up after breakfast and take her to work. I guess maybe he worked in the same place. The last time I saw her, she was getting into the car with him."

"Where was Abby working?" I asked.

Nicky fidgeted with her earring. "I don't remember. I know she'd been subbing at an orthodontist's office, but that might have ended. I wish I could remember. Half the time, I can't keep my schedule straight."

"Is that how you two met?" Fennel asked.

Nicky nodded. "We started out at the same temp agency, A La Carte Hires. They might know where she was working."

Fennel didn't tell her that was the first place we checked. According to the agency, Abigail Booker hadn't been placed in a job in over a month. Wherever she was working, if she was working, she was doing it off the books, and she hadn't told her friend about it.

Nicky looked at the photo again, stabbing it with a manicured nail. "I know that's the guy. He had these thick, black frames, and his hair was combed differently. But it's him. I swear." Her focus darted from Fennel to me. "Do you need me to sign a statement or something? You are going to arrest him, right? He must know where Abby is."

"We'll let you know if we need you," I promised.

"But what about the guy? You have his picture. You must know who he is. You gotta find out what he did to Abby."

"What makes you think he's involved?" Fennel asked.

Nicky stared, her mouth agape, as if my partner was the stupidest man alive. "Well, if he isn't, why didn't he report Abby missing? She couldn't go an entire hour without texting him. He probably noticed the moment she disappeared, which is why I think he did something to her. I watch those true crime shows. He could have her locked in a basement or worse." She pulled more vehemently on her earring. "You gotta find her."

"We'll do our best," Fennel said. "And I promise you, this guy will get what he deserves."

Her eyes went hard, and she nodded slowly. "I'm holding you to that."

SEVEN

Fennel hung up the phone. "Keith Richardson, or whatever the hell his real name is, was at the restaurant where Lyla James works. He was on the security cam footage. He came in every day the week before she disappeared and always sat in her section."

"He requested it," I said.

"Yeah, but he never spoke to the other waitress." Brad scratched his cheek. "What was her name?"

"Bethany."

He snapped his fingers. "Yeah. So why was Lyla so special?"

A sick thought had been gnawing at me ever since we spoke to Nicky. "Where are his other victims?"

"Liv, don't go there yet. We don't have any proof he did anything to Lyla or Abigail."

I hated when Brad tried to coddle me with his optimistic bullshit. "So where the hell are they?" I shuffled through the papers cluttering my desk. "And where is the damned coroner's report?" I pushed away from the desk. "Fuck this. I'm going to see what kinds of trace CSU pulled from that prick's belongings. It has to shed some light on where he came from and where he's been. We need to move on this now."

Storming out of the bullpen, I took the stairs, my thoughts moving faster than my feet. Why those women? Were we dealing with a serial killer? Obviously, the bastard had a screw loose. He said someone made him shoot Jane Doe, and that same person made him jump off the roof. A lot of whack jobs heard voices. Son of Sam received cosmic messages from a dog. Maybe this guy listened to his cat or canary.

The crime scene techs did their best to assist, but they didn't find much on the man we knew as Keith Richardson. He had DNA from three people on his clothes, Jane Doe, me, and his own. They didn't find any other samples, so if he had gone on a murderous rampage, he showered and changed in between the killings. His clothing was basic, everyday wear that could be purchased from any mall. The dirt and grime on his shoes didn't indicate anything special. He'd been walking around the city, just like everyone else.

"What about his phone?" I picked up an evidence bag and shifted the fragments around. Nicky said he and Abigail texted, but Abigail's phone records showed messages to an unregistered burner. Could this be the same phone?

"It can't be salvaged."

I squeezed my eyes closed and bit back a curse. "What about a metro card or one of those stupid smart watches? Anything?"

"Sorry, Detective. You'll have to work this one the hard way."

"What do you think I've been doing?"

The tech raised an eyebrow.

"I'm sorry. Thanks for trying. What about Jane Doe? Anything on her?"

"She's a bit more interesting." He held up a gold bracelet. "We found this. Based on her build, she might have been a dancer."

I examined the ballet slipper charm hanging from the bracelet. "Anything else?"

"It's probably nothing, but we found this next to the dumpster, near the body. We're not sure it's hers." He held out another evidence bag, and I looked at the miniature snow globe of Berlin. I flipped it over, but the few words on the worn label were written in German. "Her prints were on it, but maybe she touched it before she died."

"Or she was carrying it when she was killed." I put the bag down beside the bracelet.

"I'm sorry I don't have more answers for you."

"That makes two of us." I apologized again for my outburst. "At least two women are still missing. We need to find them."

The tech nodded, but when I left, I heard him mumble to himself, "Then maybe you shouldn't have let the killer fall off the roof."

Yeah, I thought, *too late now.*

Fennel looked up when I approached the desk. "I just got off the phone with Carrie. The coroner is going to start Richardson's autopsy in a few hours."

"About damn time."

Brad nodded. "The captain wants to see you."

"Great." Nonplussed, I crossed to his office and knocked on the door. Grayson waved me inside and told me to shut the door. "Sir?"

"Take a seat, Liv. Detective Fennel told me the abductions and our jumper are connected."

"Some jumper. He's a killer." I leaned forward in the chair, my elbows resting on my knees while my right leg jittered up and down. The unspoken assumption hung heavily in the air between us. The women we'd been desperately searching for were probably dead, killed by that bastard. "A coward really. He was too afraid to face the consequences, so he took the easy way out."

Captain Grayson cleared his throat. "Internal affairs didn't find you at fault, but they brought some things to my attention that we should talk about."

"Now's not a great time. We're behind the eight ball on this case. We have been since the moment we caught it." I moved to stand, but he put a hand up to stop me.

"Sit down, DeMarco. I didn't dismiss you."

"Sorry, sir." I sat up straight, feeling like I'd been called to the principal's office.

"Your work undercover is exemplary, but it's led to some bad habits. And you need to break them fast. You have a partner for a reason. He trusts you to have his back, so you need to let him have yours."

"But, Captain," I tried to interrupt but Grayson silenced me with a wave of his hand.

"I don't care what IA decided. You shouldn't have been up on that roof alone. And if a suspect pulls a gun, you damn well better clear leather. Do I make myself clear?"

"Yes, sir."

He sighed. "Until I'm sure you'll take these lessons to heart, you don't go anywhere without Fennel. If you have to take a leak, he'll stand in the ladies' room and hold your handbag. Is that understood?"

"Absolutely." I glanced uncertainly at Grayson. "May I go?"

"Yeah, go. But, Liv, I refuse to tell Vince something happened to his only daughter, so you will not put me in that position."

"Yes, sir. Understood."

Frustrated, I returned to my desk. Laura 'Mac' Mackenzie sent the business profiles to my drop box. For the next few hours, I read the details and ran additional searches. With any luck, Keith Richardson worked at one of these places. Of course, since that wasn't his name, I had to look through the employee databases, and a lot of those weren't public. I made some calls, but no one wanted to cooperate. We'd need a court order. I just didn't know if we had enough to get one.

"Logan Winters," the ADA greeted, "attorney extraordinaire and part-time miracle worker. How may I help you?"

"Do you always answer the phone like that?"

"Only when you call, Detective."

"How'd you know it was me?"

"I'm clairvoyant and know how to read a caller ID."

I looked down at my desk phone. "I didn't realize you knew the number. Anyway, do I need to press two for miracle worker. Exactly how does this work?"

"Tell me what the problem is."

So I did.

"It might be a tough sell, but since you have a witness who claims one of the missing women met the killer while at work, I'll get the records for you if you can come up with a reasonable list of places Abigail Booker worked around the time she met the killer and disappeared."

"I'll send over A La Carte Hires records. According to them, she hadn't been placed in over a month, but she might have met her abductor before that. And, Winters, I need to see A La Carte's employee database too."

"No problem, but I'm adding it to your tab."

"If I remember correctly, you're the one who owes

me. Did you forget about that stakeout you roped me into?"

"Fine, deduct it from my tab. Does this make us even, Liv?"

"Not yet."

"Then let me take you to dinner. I'm going to keep asking until you agree."

"That's bordering on sexual harassment," I playfully reminded him.

"It doesn't have to be a date. It's a dinner between colleagues. Just think about it. Let me know what you decide, but I gotta jump off here. I have to prep for court and get someone to put in the paperwork for those records."

I hung up the phone and rubbed the kink in my neck. It was progress. But I couldn't help feeling we were on a clock. If the missing women weren't dead, they were in grave danger. We had to find them fast.

Brad's phone rang, and he blindly reached for it. His eyes remained glued to the intel he was analyzing. "Detective Fennel." He shot up from his chair. "What?"

Instantly, I tensed. I knew that tone. I stared with bated breath.

"What?" he repeated.

My eyes darted around the room, but I didn't notice any signs of danger. No one else seemed nearly as perturbed. This was an isolated incident, specific only to my partner. My mind went to worst case scenarios.

"Don't do anything. Don't touch anything. I'll be right there." He hung up the phone, grabbed his gun from his desk drawer, and put it in his holster.

"What is it?"

"The bodies are gone. Jane Doe and Keith Richardson. They're gone."

EIGHT

Officers cordoned off the medical examiner's office. Mac and several computer whizzes scraped the feeds while Fennel and I questioned the employees. Security was tight. Bodies came and went, but stringent protocols were in place.

"How did two bodies just vanish?" I asked Carrie.

Flummoxed, she shook her head. "I don't know, DeMarco. Keith Richardson came in two nights ago. CSU assisted on removing his belongings and cataloging the items. They filled out the paperwork, followed the proper chain of custody, and took those items with them. Given the condition of the body, the ME's assistant performed the preliminary exam, assigned the body to a drawer, and that was it. With our current backlog, we didn't get much further than that."

"What about Jane Doe? She would have been brought in sometime yesterday. Blonde. Young."

Nodding, Carrie clicked a few keys. "Nothing odd with that one either. Radner got farther in her exam since she was easier to evaluate." She pulled a folder from a filing cabinet. "I sent a copy to Detective Fennel."

"I know. I've seen it." No signs of sexual assault. Dental molds had been taken. Cause of death appeared to be fatal gunshot wounds to the chest. "But this doesn't answer my question."

"I can't answer your question because I don't know the answer."

I looked down at the logs. "I need a list of everyone who's been in and out." I read the names. "Is it possible there's been a mix-up?"

"I don't know."

I was getting really tired of that answer. "Do me a favor, check the rest of the drawers. Let's make sure no one was improperly filed."

"We already looked. But we'll check again." She pushed away from the desk and opened the door. Fennel and Radner, the autopsy technician, were already double checking the reports and contents of the drawers.

Brad turned at the sound of the door opening. He gave a slight headshake. "Everyone else is present and accounted for. No extra bodies or incorrect bodies have turned up." He held up the fingerprint scanner. "We're double checking the tags, just to make sure. It wouldn't hurt to call the mortuaries and crematoriums. According to this, several bodies have been picked up since Richardson and Doe were delivered."

"I'm on it," Carrie promised, stepping out of the frigid room.

"Mac's scrubbing the footage. And the other techs are checking the data for any anomalies. Is anything else missing?" I asked.

Radner closed another drawer. "I don't know."

"That's not what I want to hear." I met Brad's eyes.

"When you're finished, meet me in the other lab. Let's make sure nothing else vanished."

"That seems to be the theme of this case."

Carrie buzzed me into the office where files and evidence for processing were kept. Based on a brief glance, everything appeared to be in order, but appearances could be deceiving. I scanned the sheet for our case numbers and opened the drawer for the coordinating files. I found the fingerprint cards stuffed into the master files.

"Hey," Fennel rubbed his hands up and down his arms, trying to get warm, "how's it looking?"

"The files are here." I didn't see any notations on our contact lens question or hits on the dental records. "Radner, where do you keep the dental molds?"

The assistant went to a high cabinet and rolled out a tray. "Uh, Detectives, you're not going to like this." He stepped away to show us the empty slots.

"This wasn't a filing error." Brad examined the rest of the drawer, but everything else was where it should be. "Who had access to this room?"

Radner shrugged. "Only authorized personnel. I don't recall any visitors in the last couple of days."

"Have you been on second shift all week?" I asked, and Radner nodded. "All right, we'll have to check with first and third and see what they say."

"Brad," Carrie called, and we both turned to look out the open door, "I just got off the phone with the chief. The Feds were here yesterday. They took custody of two bodies late last night. Maybe they've taken over your case."

"No, they didn't." I held up the chain of custody form. "If they did, where's the transfer order?"

Carrie shrugged.

"I'll make a call," Fennel offered.

This didn't sit right with me. Not bothering to wait for proof, I headed down the hall and nearly collided with Mac. She had a tablet in hand and looked about as frantic as I felt.

"Who did this?" I asked.

She let out an uneasy laugh. "You always make me feel like I'm late to the party." She held out the device. "These guys came into the morgue right at shift change. With their cheap suits and sunglasses, you'd think someone would have found that odd."

"They timed it just right." I watched the two men enter a few seconds after Radner left. At that time of night, no one covered the desk. The men slipped into the morgue. Cameras didn't cover the autopsy room, but a few minutes later, they each rolled out a gurney, topped with a body bag. "Right there." I pointed. "How'd they get inside?"

"They had an access card." Mac opened a second tab and showed me the logs. "It's a duplicate of Dr. Emerson's card."

"How could they dupe the chief medical examiner's ID card?"

"With the right equipment, they could have pulled the data remotely, y'know like credit card thieves."

"But this wouldn't just be numbers. They'd need to recreate the actual card or the strip."

"It could be programmed in, like the way hotels code their keys. Unfortunately, it's not as difficult to get your hands on one of those machines as you might think."

"Technology, gotta love it." I tapped the screen and let the security footage resume. "So these two schmucks waltz in here, impersonate federal agents, and walk out with our jumper and his victim. Tell me you know who they are."

"Not yet," she paused the feed, "but Dr. Emerson

caught them in the act. And the exterior cameras got a good look at their van." She zoomed in. "Government plates." This was making less and less sense. "Are they real?"

"I've already run them." She dug a slip of paper out of her jacket pocket. "According to this, the van's registered to the local FBI field office." Before I could ask the obvious question, she said, "I don't know, Liv. They might be Feds, but why the secrecy? And why the sunglasses?"

"They're not Feds. Feds wouldn't use a cloned access card to steal the bodies. They'd come in, flash their badges, and take over, like they always do."

Fennel came down the hall. "I just got off the phone. The Bureau doesn't know anything about this. The department liaison is checking with the other agencies, but I doubt we'll get a hit. The case would be kicked without filing the proper documentation. I think we're dealing with a couple of body snatchers."

"You didn't happen to ask the Bureau if they were missing one of their vans, did you?" I asked.

Fennel quirked an eyebrow. "I didn't know I was supposed to." Mac caught him up to speed, and when she was done, he whistled. "Let's question Doc Emerson. I'll have a sketch artist meet us. Hopefully, that'll be enough to ID these guys."

"In the meantime, I'll run this through facial rec. But with their reflective glasses, it won't be an exact science," Mac said. "We probably won't get a hit."

"Do your best." I shook my head. "Am I the only person who thinks men wearing sunglasses in the middle of the night is suspicious?"

"No, but maybe Dr. Emerson isn't as observant as you are." Fennel passed along orders to a couple of nearby uniforms, said goodbye to Carrie, and led the way back to the car.

"Are you okay?" I asked.

"Yeah, why?"

"You were starting to look a little green. I know you don't like bodies or body snatchers."

He graced me with a smile. "I knew you'd think that was funny."

"You need to work on your material."

"Who has the time?" He sobered. "You're right though. I don't like this part of the job, but no one does." He programmed Dr. Emerson's home address into the nav system. "Apparently, we've graduated from missing persons to missing bodies. What's next?"

"I don't want to know, but it better not be an alien invasion. Or I'm blaming you."

NINE

"It's done," the voice on the other end of the line said.

He took a breath. It felt like the first time since he heard of Keith's demise. "Are you positive the bodies won't be discovered?"

"They've been disposed of. Nothing's left. We took the molds and wiped the system. No one will ever discover their true identities. You're in the clear."

"Excellent. What about the van? Did you have any problems getting it or returning it?"

"Not one. The access codes you gave us worked like a charm. We got in and out and avoided the security cameras."

"And the front gate?" he asked, fearing his two foreign associates could be identified.

"We did as you said and wore the costumes you provided. Suits, sunglasses," Oleg laughed, "we looked ridiculous, but no one thought anything of it. We wore gloves. We were careful not to leave any trace inside. Should they discover the van went missing for a few hours, they'll just think a couple of agents checked it out and forgot to fill out the paperwork. There's nothing to worry about. Your access codes and ID cards worked like a charm."

"All right. Keep out of sight. I'll need you and Dmitri to guard the girls for the next few days."

"It'll cost you."

"I know."

He needed to find someone to replace Keith, but now wasn't the time. He didn't necessarily trust Dmitri and Oleg, but unlike Keith, they had a vested interest in not getting caught. They worked for one of his foreign buyers. Their boss was ruthless, an old school Russian gangster who might have been former Spetsnaz or KGB, but it didn't matter now. The man had money and brought in a lot of business. He'd do whatever it took to keep his Russian buyer happy, and Dmitri and Oleg would do the same if they wanted to remain breathing. He could trust them to guard the girls. After all, several of them would be handed over to the Russian soon enough.

* * *

"Tell me that did not just happen." I handed the keys to Fennel and slid into the passenger seat. "I can't deal with any more stupid people today. The Bureau better be on their toes because I might lose it. Maybe we should reschedule that sick day you talked about. Chicken soup and cartoons sounds nice, doesn't it? We could let Loyola and Sullivan handle this."

"I wish." My partner adjusted the seat and fixed the mirrors. "How the hell did Emerson become chief medical examiner? When he asked those two FBI impersonators what they were doing with the bodies, he should have followed up. Apparently, anyone can walk into the morgue, steal a body or two, and walk out."

"Only if they encounter Emerson."

"Yeah, because the chief ME's gullible enough to believe anything. I can't believe he didn't make sure the paperwork was in order before letting them take the bodies. It's unbelievable. The security measures, policies, and protocols in place are designed to stop this sort of thing from happening. Isn't Emerson aware of this? Did he even read the handbook?"

"Probably not." I turned to face Brad. "The FBI imposters knew this. They waited for security to be lax. I watched the footage. The guard who just came on shift stepped away for a few seconds to grab the logbook, and that's when they entered. And since it was after hours and the door was locked, the guard had no reason to think stepping away from his post would cause any problems."

"He didn't know these thieves had a freaking key."

"Emerson's key." More questions came to mind. "They must have eyes inside the morgue. It's the only way they'd know the guard wasn't at his post." I sent a text to Mac with my suspicions. If the ME's office was breached, she'd discover it.

"Still, Emerson's to blame," Fennel insisted. "They cloned his key. He must have done something stupid that gave them access. I know he's helped in a lot of our cases, but the guy's a moron."

"It's not what you know. It's who you know or who you blow."

"According to Carrie—"

I turned, shock and disgust on my face. "Please tell me she doesn't have firsthand knowledge of Emerson's cunnilingus skills."

Brad made gagging sounds. "Liv, I so did not need that visual. Ugh." He cringed and glared at me. "You just torpedoed my sex life. The next time I see her, what do you think will go through my head? I don't need that imagery."

"Sorry."

He growled at me and narrowed his eyes. "What I was going to say," he shivered again, "before you grossed me out, was according to Carrie, Emerson's a savant when it comes to pathology. But he has zero common sense and is extremely gullible. Every April Fool's, they run a pool to see how long it'll take him to get the joke, but he never does."

"Is that why he works the night shift? To avoid dealing with people?" It would also explain why I rarely encountered the man outside of court.

"Probably."

I picked up the two sketches. Emerson's recollection provided additional details we couldn't get from the security feed, like the small mole below the guy's lip and the busted veins on the other man's cheeks. And their accents, although Emerson couldn't narrow it down to region or dialect, we knew they spoke with accents. "He's probably a drinker."

"The doc?"

"No," I flashed one of the sketches at Brad, "our chubby FBI impersonator." The other man was rail thin. "I know who they are. Laurel and Hardy."

"Aren't they dead?"

"Probably. But one's tall and thin, the other not so thin. They're both wearing suits. Can you think of any other duo who fits our description?"

"And you say I need to work on my material. Ha." He blew out a breath. "Fine. We'll go with Laurel and Hardy for now. Maybe the Feds can shed some light on this. After all, their van got jacked. They'll want to get to the bottom of it."

Of course, the FBI had no idea what we were talking about. When we started asking questions, an agent accompanied us to the garage. The van was parked on the end.

"I can't believe they returned it." I pulled a latex glove from my pocket and opened the rear door. "No sign of either body."

Fennel checked the plate and the VIN against our intel. "It's the same van."

I opened the driver's door and checked the steering column. The van hadn't been hotwired. I didn't like where this was going. Brad joined me and peered inside. He flipped down the visor and checked under the floor mat, but the keys weren't inside.

My partner turned to the agent assisting us. "This van was used in the commission of a crime. I'd like to get it processed. I'd also like to know who had it last, and I'd like to see the security footage for the garage. Can you make that happen?"

"You're certain it was this van?" Agent Peters asked.

"Positive." I held out a still photograph from the surveillance footage. "Same plates. Same VIN."

"Son of a bitch." Peters circled the vehicle. "Yeah, I'll get right on this. Let me get authorization. Wait here, Detectives."

While we waited for Peters to return, I looked around the garage. It was a far cry from the PD's motor pool. It should have been nearly impossible to steal a van and even more difficult to return it without authorization. This read like an inside job.

The garage was beneath the federal building. The entire area was under surveillance. Agents were stationed at the entrances. No one could get in or out without credentials or authorization. That realization left a growing unease in my mind.

"Are you sure no policing agency took jurisdiction of our case or our victims?"

Fennel blinked a few times. He saw the same things I did. "They all denied it. Unless Richardson or Doe were assets or undercover agents, they'd have no reason to lie about it. Captain Grayson said he'd make sure we weren't getting the runaround."

"It looks like we are."

Agent Peters returned with another man he introduced as Director Kendall, the head of the field office. We shook hands and updated Kendall on the situation, hoping he'd clue us in as to how or why someone took possession of an FBI van and absconded with two bodies.

"I'm sorry, Detectives. It wasn't us." Kendall frowned. "We'd prefer to investigate this matter ourselves. However, I've spoken to the police commissioner, and we've agreed to a joint investigation. When these bastards stole our van, they dragged us into this. I don't want to step on any toes. I just want to know how two men came into my garage, borrowed my van, and returned it without anyone noticing. Send a team to help us process and evaluate the scene. We'll share our findings. I'd appreciate it if you do the same."

"Thank you, Director." Fennel nodded while I made the call.

Once a team of police investigators arrived, Fennel and I left the federal building more confused than before we arrived. Why would someone steal the bodies? What were they trying to conceal? And how did this connect to our four missing women? The only people with direct access were federal agents. I didn't like where this investigation was heading.

"Our suspects knew when to strike. They knew the security weaknesses at the ME's office. They knew how to get an official van from the federal building without being caught or questioned. And they returned it, so no one would know."

Brad glanced at me. "Someone on the job made those bodies disappear."

"It's the only thing that makes sense."

"All right. Why do it? Richardson killed Doe then himself. What did Laurel and Hardy think we'd find on the bodies?"

"Drugs?" I speculated. I didn't know what else would be uncovered in an autopsy that we didn't already know about.

"Maybe, but with the way our jumper went splat," Fennel's words brought the image back into my mind, and I inhaled sharply, "if he was a mule, the balloons would have ruptured. There might be trace in the blood and tissue samples taken."

"Do we still have those? The FBI imposters, or whoever the hell they are, they stole the dental molds."

"I'll check when we get inside." Fennel pulled into a space and grinned. "But I bet that's why they took the bodies. They don't want us to identify them. It's why they stole the dental molds and wiped the search."

"But why?" Even as I asked the question, I knew this had to do with the reason Richardson jumped off the roof. "Someone orchestrated all of this. The abductions. The murder. And stealing the bodies. And whoever it is has power. And he wants to cover up his involvement."

"Like a dirty FBI agent?"

"I don't know. But it's someone at the top of the food chain. We need to find out who."

As requested, the business records and employee manifests were waiting at my desk. ADA Winters left a note, reminding me he worked another miracle. I pushed it to the side. There were a dozen stacks, neatly sorted and individually clipped. These were the employee manifests and business records for Abigail Booker's temp jobs.

Starting with A La Carte Hires, I began my search for Keith Richardson or whatever name he might be using. A La Carte Hires had hundreds of temps in their candidate pool. This would take days to properly assess, but to save time, I sorted the stacks, removing anyone who fit Keith Richardson or Jane Doe's description.

Since Richardson didn't work for A La Carte Hires and wasn't listed in their pool, I moved on to sorting the remaining records in chronological order from Booker's most recent gig to her least recent. But none of them looked promising. Nicky said Abigail met Keith only a few days before she disappeared. It was unlikely they crossed paths more than a month ago.

Luckily, Winters convinced a judge to compel Rogers and Stein and several other offices in the vicinity to hand over their records in regards to Jane Doe's murder. Since the receptionist thought she recognized Jane Doe, Winters convinced a judge that was enough.

I organized those business records by location and proximity to the body and started at the top. My gut said the modeling agency was our best bet, but gut instinct wasn't enough to get warrants or make arrests. So I took my time. The answer was here. It had to be.

"The tox screen came back for Richardson," Fennel said. "Alcohol and marijuana. Nothing else."

"That's not helpful." I placed another set of records off to the side. "What about the contact lenses?"

"Radner didn't note any, so he doesn't think Richardson wore contacts. It's not definitive, but it's our best guess. However, if Richardson had his eyes open on the way down, the force of the wind might have displaced the lenses in his eyes, and–"

"I don't need you to finish that statement. I'm queasy enough." I reached into the bottom drawer and pulled out a bag of ginger chews. "Do you want one? You've been looking green all day."

"No." Fennel reached for a stack of files. "Until Mac or the crime techs find something, I might as well help with the paperwork. We have plenty to keep us busy."

"I'm just checking the records for any employee who matches Richardson or Doe."

"You think Abigail Booker worked with Jane Doe?"

"I have no idea, but that's never stopped me before."

We spent hours combing through the files and data. Only a handful of companies took employee photos. None of them matched anyone of interest. Without knowing actual names or having a list of aliases, we had to enter each name into the DMV database to get a photo. And that took time. This was why my father always said police work was 90% paperwork.

"DeMarco, phone. Line two," an officer said.

"Thanks." I picked up my desk phone and pressed a button. "Detective DeMarco speaking."

"This is Agent Peters. I just wanted to let you know we've processed the van. No prints. No hairs. No fibers. Nothing indicates who took it or what they used it for."

We know what they used it for. "Okay."

"The men who impersonated agents and stole the van disabled the onboard navigation system, but they didn't disable the internal tracking system. After they left the ME's office, they detoured to the warehouse district. I'm guessing they dumped the bodies there."

"Give me the address." I scribbled it down.

"We've already sent a team of agents," Peters said.

"And a few of the PD's crime techs are along for the ride. We'll let you know what we find. I just wanted to update you."

"Thanks."

Hanging up, I took the address and went into Captain Grayson's office to tell him what was going on. However, he didn't want to send any more officers to help in the search, and he ordered me to stay at my desk and work the intel. The same went for Fennel. Apparently, I was in the doghouse.

By the time I looked up from the paperwork, I couldn't even see straight. Fennel keyed in another entry, sighed, and went to the next name on the list. When he realized I wasn't working, he stopped and leaned back in his chair.

"Calling it quits?"

"Not yet. I'm not giving up until I figure out how Keith Richardson connects to Abigail. Once we find that, we might be able to draw a line between him and the two missing prostitutes. He has to connect to the others. Nicky IDed him." I thought for a moment. "How did he find these women? Why did he pick them?"

"The better question is how did he know to pick them." Brad grabbed the baseball off his desk and tossed it in the air. "According to Nicky, Booker met Richardson at work and they started dating. From the security footage we've seen, Richardson ate at the restaurant where Lyla worked. We know how he connects to our two missing persons. And since he found them, it wouldn't have been hard for him to find a couple of streetwalkers. The question we should ask is how did he know to pick those specific women."

"What do you mean?"

Fennel continued to toss the ball in the air. "C'mon, Liv. Think about it. The pros were easy. Most don't have homes or families or regular jobs. So no one would notice if they disappeared, and if someone did, well," he glanced around, "missing persons didn't exactly start a citywide search to find them. He knew they wouldn't be a priority. Anyone with two functioning brain cells would realize that. But most college students would be missed. But he picked Lyla James. No family ties. No strong connections. That's why it took a week before anyone reported her missing."

"And if it hadn't been for Nicky, no one would have known Abigail disappeared either." When we tried to follow up with Booker's next of kin, we didn't find any. And since she was out of work and never had a steady gig to begin with, she didn't have a boss to report her missing either. "Damn, you're a genius."

"I know." Catching the ball, he rocked forward and placed it on the stand. "So you should take me to dinner."

I cocked an eyebrow at him. "Do you have somewhere special in mind?"

"I do."

TEN

"The modeling agency is still our best bet." I skewered a slice of avocado and popped it into my mouth. "Keith Richardson didn't work at Rogers and Stein, but the agency hires a lot of freelancers. Photographers, mostly. And they see dozens of women every day. It makes the most sense. That's probably where Keith met Jane."

Fennel poked at his salad, his eyes constantly roaming the restaurant. "Lyla worked here. It's close enough to the modeling agency for Richardson's daily lunch trips to be feasible, if he even worked there, but that's assuming a lot. You're guessing he did some kind of freelance work for them and that Jane Doe was one of their models or auditioning to be a model."

"Speculation is all we have right now. Do you have a better theory?"

"Have you looked around?"

I turned my head. The place wasn't upscale, and the menu didn't offer much in variety. It was a mid-level restaurant and dry. As a rule, executives and models both enjoyed drinking.

"No one at Rogers and Stein would have recommended this place. Hell, I doubt they even know it exists." Something out the window caught Brad's eye. "Maybe we're looking at this all wrong. I agree. Richardson must have known things about the women he abducted and the one he killed, assuming, of course, he's behind the abductions."

"Seems like a safe bet."

Brad nodded, continuing to follow his train of thought. "But maybe they didn't have work in common. Nicky could have gotten it wrong. She didn't even know Abigail had been out of work for a month, so we shouldn't assume she knows how Abigail met Keith."

"Okay, so where does that put us? Back at square one?"

"Not necessarily. Two of the victims worked the streets. Lyla worked here. And Abigail worked everywhere and nowhere." He took a final bite and chewed. "The victims must have something else in common."

"We've gone over it a hundred times. Missing persons went over it too. We didn't find any commonalities. I'm not even sure the four victims are connected. And without knowing more about Jane Doe, we can't exactly build a profile on her." I pulled a pen out of my purse and reached for a clean napkin. "Okay, let's toss out anything we can't solidly connect."

"Prostitutes are gone."

"Right." I wrote our jumper's name in the middle. "Keith dated Abigail Booker. So we keep her. He ate at this restaurant for a week prior to Lyla James's disappearance. So she stays. And ballistics matched the gun, so he killed Jane Doe."

"And we know Laurel and Hardy impersonated FBI

agents, broke into the morgue, and stole the bodies."

"Yeah." I continued drawing lines from the names to additional pieces of evidence we possessed. The gun. The stolen van. The snow globe. The gold bracelet and charm. "Laurel and Hardy have accents. That's what Emerson said."

"For all we know, they could be from Texas."

"Or Germany. Emerson wasn't particularly forthcoming." I glanced at my phone. Agent Peters hadn't called back. Mac and the techs were split between processing the ME's office and assisting the FBI in determining how the garage was breached. The men were caught on camera, but they had convincing fake FBI credentials. How did they get those? "Are we sure the Bureau isn't screwing with us?"

Brad reached into his wallet. Since I bought dinner, he left the tip. "I'm not sure of anything." He jerked his chin out the window. "It's a nice night. Let's take a walk. And depending on how that goes, maybe we'll take a drive to the warehouse district and see how Agent Peters is faring."

"The captain won't be happy about that."

"He doesn't need to know." Fennel kept his focus out the window. Something had caught his attention.

I stuffed the napkin into my bag and grabbed my phone. "Do you have a theory? Or a destination?"

"I'm working on it."

We left the restaurant and strolled down the street. We were only a few blocks from where we conducted surveillance a few nights ago. Grayson assigned Sullivan and Loyola to keep watch for anything hinky in our absence. However, the streets appeared quiet, but it was still early. We turned at the next intersection and stopped in front of the community center.

"None of our victims were financially solvent. They

were scraping by. Maybe they needed a hand," Brad suggested.

"Lyla was doing okay."

"She was a student. I've seen her bills. Most of her expenses were covered by student loans. What she earned at the restaurant went for incidentals and outside acting classes." He read the sign on the door. "For Richardson to realize our victims were easy prey, he'd have to be paying attention or the women volunteered the information."

"What are you thinking? Soup kitchen, shelters, free clinics, that sort of thing? They weren't exactly indigent. All four of them have known addresses. They didn't need a handout." Although, I didn't know how reliable our intel was when it came to the working girls. "And Lyla worked at a restaurant. That place might not be the best, but she could have gotten scraps or leftovers to take home."

Brad gave me a sideways glance and pointed at the window. "Free health screenings and physicals."

"So?"

"None of them had health insurance."

"Lyla could have gone to the clinic on campus." Medical records were harder to come by due to privacy laws, so I couldn't be certain of my assertion.

"Sure, if she was sick or needed birth control. But she needed to have a physical to participate in community theater. And since this place is close to where she acted and worked, she might have come here instead."

"This is a stretch, Fennel."

"It won't hurt to ask around. We've checked everywhere else." Even though it was late, he pushed the door open. I frowned, wondering why the community center wasn't locked up tight. As if reading my mind, Brad pointed to the sign. *AA meeting – room 103.*

"They won't talk to us." It was the nature of AA. Answering our questions would defeat the anonymous part.

"Sure, they will." He grinned. "You're afraid I have a problem, so I think I should go to a meeting, just to make sure I don't. If nothing else, it'll put your mind at ease." He winked. "And I love proving you wrong."

"This is such a bad idea," I mumbled, following Brad down the hall and into the meeting.

They started forty minutes ago, so we ducked into the room and found unobtrusive seats near the back. When they were finished, the man in charge approached us. He introduced himself as David, disrupting the illusion of true anonymity. But I didn't point out the hypocrisy.

"I'm Brad. This is my partner, Liv."

"Welcome," David shook hands with each of us, believing Brad and I were romantically involved, "I haven't seen you here before."

"First time," Brad said.

"Do you normally attend a different meeting?" David asked.

"No," Brad looked at me, "we just stepped in on a whim. Liv's afraid my drinking is out of control, so we're trying to be proactive."

"We should talk." David eyed me curiously. "Help yourself to coffee and donuts."

I gave Brad a curious look. This would give me a chance to question the others, but I wasn't sure he was prepared to be cornered about a potential problem that he probably didn't even have. Honestly, he said he was fine, but I still worried about him. Maybe he had a problem, and this was killing two birds with one stone. Or maybe I was overthinking our cover.

"Go on, hun. Grab a coffee. One for me too, please." Brad jerked his chin at the table. "You know how I take it."

I shuffled away, eyeing the two dozen remaining people. They broke into small groups of two to three, hiding behind their coffee cups and donuts. Addiction came in plenty of forms. Even though this was an alcoholics anonymous meeting, I wasn't convinced a few of them hadn't dabbled with other vices. Regardless, it was refreshing to see people actively trying to better their lives and recover.

I smiled at two women as I moved to the table in the back. Grabbing a paper cup from the stack, I placed it under the spout. With the cup three-quarters full, I examined the sweeteners.

"Pink, blue, yellow, or white?" a man said, stepping up beside me. He grabbed several white packets and tore off the tops before dumping them into a cup and snagging a glazed donut. He gave me the quick once-over. "Wait. Don't tell me. Let me guess. Blue?"

"Actually, I was hoping for brown."

His forehead wrinkled. "Brown?"

"Raw sugar."

"Ah, a purist." He put the donut in his mouth to free up one of his hands and dug through the packets, pulling out four from the bottom. After handing them to me, he took the donut out of his mouth. "Will that do?"

"That's plenty. Thank you."

"No problem." He turned his back to the table and surveyed the room. "Place was starting to empty out. Glad to see some new faces. I'm Jesse, by the way."

"Liv." I watched a few people wander out. "It looks like a good-sized crowd. How many people usually show up?"

"I dunno. Thirty. Thirty-five." He took another bite

of his donut. "I got my ninety-day chip today."

"Congratulations."

He snickered. "A part of me wants to celebrate with a few beers. Isn't that crazy?"

"No, but it's not a good idea."

"Yeah, I know. So it's burnt coffee and a soggy donut." He glanced back at the nearly empty box. "You might want to grab one before the rest disappear."

"I don't do grains."

"That would make giving up drinking a lot easier. God, what's left? Wine?"

I shrugged.

"You ever hang out around here?" Jesse asked. "I do some volunteer work for the community center. Charity drives, bake sales, stuff like that."

"I can't say that I do."

"I probably wouldn't either, except it's court-mandated. It's why I started coming to this meeting."

I turned to face him. "Do you know Keith?"

Jesse chewed on the last piece of his donut and wiped his mouth with his thumb. "You mean Tobias? Tobias Keith? He works the front desk." He reached for another donut and studied my expression.

"Maybe. What does he look like?"

"He's like this tall." He gestured with the donut. "Dark hair. Glasses. Thin, like lean muscle thin, like runner thin. Not sick thin or addict thin. Just thin."

"That sounds like him. What did you say his name was?"

"Tobias Keith. Y'know, kind of like the singer. I used to give him a hard time about it every time I saw him." Jesse took another bite and spoke with his mouth full. "Come to think of it, I haven't seen him in a couple of days."

"Does he normally come to these meetings?"

"Nah. He just works the front desk. Is that how you heard the meeting moved here?"

My brain remained two steps behind, which wasn't good for a cop. "You mean this is new?"

Jesse laughed. "Yeah, we started up eight weeks ago. I used to attend the meeting they held in the church on Seventh, but they closed down. So that's when the community center started holding it here. And since I was already in the area, it made sense to just stick around." He finished his donut and took a sip of coffee.

"How long has Tobias worked here?"

"I don't know."

"Do you know Lyla James?"

My questions were making him suspicious. "How long have you been clean and sober?"

"Um," I thought back, "the last time I had a drink was three and a half weeks ago." Which wasn't a lie. I just wasn't a big drinker. "One day at a time, right?"

Finding my answer satisfactory, Jesse said, "Yeah, I know Lyla. Everyone here knows Lyla. She plastered every bulletin board in this building with posters for her upcoming show." He rolled his eyes. "She's delusional to think anyone here gives a shit, but she's convinced it's her big break. Poor kid. She acts like she's opening on Broadway. She doesn't realize it's fucking community theater." He pressed his fingers to his lips. "Pardon my language."

"What about–"

He drained his cup and tossed it in the trash. "I get it. You're new. But this is AA. It's not about gossip or asking about other people. You need someone to talk to about your problems, I'm here to listen. But if not, I gotta bounce."

"Yeah, sure. I get it." I held up the raw sugar packets. "Thanks for this."

He bowed his head and went to speak to a woman with raven-colored hair on the other side of the room. Tobias Keith. Keith Richardson. Dammit. I was losing my touch or extremely dense. Keith Richards. Toby Keith. The jumper must have been a music fan. He probably thought he was clever to come up with those aliases. He probably got a kick out of the fake IDs too. But that no longer mattered.

First, we needed to make sure Tobias was the same man who plummeted from the roof. It looked like this may have been our abductor's hunting ground. We'd need to ask questions, but since the rest of the center was shut down for the night, it'd have to wait until the morning.

I shook one of the sugar packets and tore off the top before pouring it into the cup. This new information left me jittery enough. The last thing I needed was coffee, but Brad might want one. And now that I had a potential lead, it was time to leave. I wandered back to Fennel and David.

"Here, honey."

Brad took the cup and shook hands with David. "Thanks for the information."

"No problem. I hope to see you again."

Brad didn't say anything. He just nodded and placed a hand on the small of my back, guiding me to the door. On the way out, I snagged a flyer from a bulletin board.

When we were safely outside, I asked, "Are you okay?"

"If you keep asking me that, I might start thinking I don't look very okay." He eyed me. "Do I not look okay?"

"You look fine."

"Only fine?"

I elbowed him in the ribs. "Fishing for

compliments?"

"Just the truth." He stopped near a parked car and checked his reflection in the window. "Don't you think I'm handsome?"

"Not this again." I dragged him away from the car. "Did you get anything useful out of the AA meeting?"

"David didn't say anything. He wouldn't confirm any regular attendees, but I don't think Lyla or Abigail had a drinking problem. I'll ask Nicky the next time we follow up, but I think she would have mentioned it. Plus, most addicts have a tendency to disappear, beg, borrow, and steal. And Lyla and Abigail don't fit the bill."

"Lyla disappeared from time to time." I remembered her coworkers mentioning that. "And Jesse recognized her. Although, he said it was from the posters." I handed the flyer to Brad. "But it is possible she could have gone to a few meetings, and he wanted to maintain her anonymity. He takes that very seriously."

After filling my partner in on everything I learned, we drove to the warehouse district to check on the progress the Feds were making. We needed a win. Even though Brad and I made some headway in discovering where and how Keith Richardson chose his victims, it wasn't enough. We needed more. A lot more. But at least now we knew where to look for answers.

ELEVEN

"You said no one would find the bodies," he bellowed.

"They didn't."

He slammed his office door. He didn't need anyone to overhear his conversation. "So why are the police and FBI scouring the buildings in the warehouse district?"

"The van." Oleg poured a drink and sipped deeply. The liquor warmed his body, and he leaned back, balancing the glass on his thigh. "You told us to deactivate the nav system, but the FBI must have other trackers on their vehicles. Did you forget? Maybe you made another mistake?"

He swore. He'd forgotten about the satellite tracking. "What will they find?"

"Ash."

"That's it?" He needed the reassurance now more than ever. For a moment, he thought about his golden parachute. He could pull the ripcord, take the small fortune he'd accumulated, and run. He had contacts in Brazil. His buyers there were far more forgiving than the Russians. They might hide him or protect him, especially based on how much he was willing to pay. He could set up shop down there. It wouldn't be nearly as easy, but he could do it. He still had enough friends to make things happen.

"You should speak to Dmitri. He took over the disposal."

Dmitri was a professional. He'd seen the man's work before. He used him a time or two when things had gotten out of hand. Accidents occasionally happened. Prospective buyers didn't always understand the rules or the consequences. And less often, the girls stepped out of line and had to be dealt with. Dmitri always handled those incidents, and nothing had ever bounced back on any of them.

"All right. Thanks."

Oleg chuckled. "Not so fast. You realize my boss still expects a nubile blonde. A natural blonde."

"I haven't forgotten."

"She needs to be ready by tomorrow. You know what happens if you don't follow through."

He leafed through a file on his desk. "Hold on." He stepped into the hallway. As usual, the office was busy. "Vera, bring me the file on Clarissa Berens. I need to see something."

"My boss is not a patient man. And you're already under the gun," the voice on the other end of the line said.

"It's Keith's fault. He let Ingrid get away. I couldn't risk taking her back after the escape. I didn't know who she'd seen or spoken to. She could have jeopardized everything. She could have shown the others how she escaped." He abruptly stopped speaking when his assistant entered with the file. He took it from her and offered a polite smile. She returned the smile and left his office, closing the door behind her. "Can't you explain the situation to your boss? He needs to understand this isn't my fault. I need more time."

"He won't understand. You know how this works."

He read the file. No one would miss Clarissa Berens. The girl had a terrible life, but she had one thing going for her. She was a natural blonde. "Okay. I have someone in mind, but you'll have to make the pick-up. Make sure it's a clean grab."

"Protect the girls. Grab the girls. I'm wondering why we need you."

"Never mind. I'll take care of it. She'll be delivered to the usual exchange spot. He can look over the merchandise and make his purchases."

"Very good."

Hanging up, he rocked back in his chair. He had a list of associates, but with the police sniffing around, he'd been hesitant to enlist any of them. Unfortunately, he no longer had a choice. He dug the burner phone out of his bottom desk drawer and dialed a number.

*　　*　　*

"Detectives," Agent Peters waved us through the tape, "I didn't expect to see you again tonight."

"We were in the neighborhood." I followed Peters into an abandoned processing plant, down a hallway, and into a large room with an industrial fan intended to prevent overheating. "How do you know Laurel and Hardy came in here?"

Peters gave me a strange look. "Oh," he chuckled, "I get it." In the back of the room, several men in blue coveralls and latex gloves sifted through the remnants of the incinerator. "The van pulled into the loading bay. It remained for less than five minutes before returning to the federal building."

Fennel crouched down, examining the ashes and bone fragments. "How long for extra crispy?"

"This burns hot. A lot hotter than a crematorium, so I'd guess less than an hour." The tech pointed to several large bone fragments. "And they didn't break all the way down to ash, so possibly less than that."

"Where's the on/off switch?" Fennel asked.

"We dusted it. No prints." Peters looked around the abandoned plant.

"They split up," I said. "One of them stayed here. The other returned the van. Did you pull nearby CCTV feeds?"

"Detective DeMarco, I said the Bureau would share its findings. And I am a man of my word." Peters pointed to a few members of the PD's crime scene unit. "As soon as we know anything, you're my first call."

"Fine. We'll get out of your way."

"Good night, Detectives."

"Night," Brad said. When we got back to the car, he asked, "What do you think, partner?"

"Nothing good."

"Me neither. The men who took the bodies knew precisely how to get them and where to dispose of them. The FBI imposters know too much. Planned too well. They read like professional cleaners."

"But why? Keith Richardson was sloppy. He killed Jane Doe, left shell casings and bullets behind, and he had the murder weapon on his person when he committed suicide. Who would bother to go to this much trouble to clean up a killer's mess when the killer is already dead and we don't even know his real name?"

"That's what we have to find out."

I thought about what Brad said. "Concealing Keith

Richardson's identity is the only reason anyone would go to these extreme measures. Any idea why?"

"I don't know, Liv."

We remained silent for the rest of the ride. Our thoughts and theories too macabre to verbalize or share. Captain Grayson wouldn't be happy we detoured to the site of the body dump, but we needed to update him, despite the consequences. I offered to take the hit since my head was already on the chopping block.

Grayson didn't scold or reprimand. He listened, made a few notations, picked up the phone, and told me to call it a night. He didn't want his detectives to burn the candle at both ends when there was nothing to be done until evidence was collected and businesses opened.

I passed the order along, and Fennel made a note that we needed records from the community center. We'd probably start our day there, unless Agent Peters tracked down the imposters. I turned off the computer and stared at the corkboard. Photographs of the four missing women stared back at me.

"We'll find you," I promised, but the words sounded hollow.

By the time I got home that night, Emma was waiting for me. We hadn't spoken since Brad spilled the beans about the rooftop incident. I went to bed early last night to avoid seeing her when she got home from work, and I left for the station before she woke up this morning. So it was time I paid the piper.

"Hey, Em." I shut the door, flipped the deadbolt, and latched the chain. "How was work?"

Her tone was cold and bristly. "Fine."

"Cool." I kicked off my shoes and hung my purse in the closet. Removing my gun, I unloaded it and put it on the kitchen counter. "Did you eat yet?"

"Yes." She turned off the TV and came into the kitchen. "Sit down, Liv. We have to talk."

I took a seat, wondering if I should move my gun out of Emma's reach. She stood on the other side of the counter and stared at me.

"You know I love you, right? You're my family. I don't know where I'd be if it hadn't been for you and your parents." She took a deep breath and sighed. "But we can't have more mornings like the other day."

"Em, if this is about Brad eating your food, I'll make sure he doesn't do it again."

"It isn't about the food." She pulled out a stool and leaned across the counter. "This is about what he said. About what happened."

"Nothing happened."

"Don't lie to me, Liv."

"Nothing happened," I repeated, fighting to tamp down my annoyance.

"Brad was freaked out. I've never seen him like that, and the only reason he'd act like that was if something happened to you. So tell me your side of things. I'm all ears. I heard what he said and what you told him. But now I want the truth. I'm not a cop. I'm not IA. And I'm not your father. So tell me what happened."

"I'm going to bed. I can't talk about an open investigation."

"Don't give me that." She blocked my path to the bedroom.

"I followed a guy onto the roof. He intended to kill himself. I tried to stop him. In the course of the conversation, he admitted to killing someone else. He wanted me to kill him, and I wouldn't do it. When he realized he was caught, he broke free and jumped."

"I'm sorry."

"Happy?" The bitterness crept into my voice.

She tried to pull me in for a hug, but I stepped back. "He shot at you, so you would fire back. Damn. That's fucked up."

"It doesn't matter." But the voice in my head disagreed. Why didn't he kill me? Why didn't he fight back? He knew I was a cop. He already killed once, possibly many times more than that, so why didn't he kill me? Even if he'd given up on his own life, why didn't he take me out before plunging to his death? "He never wanted to kill her."

"What?" Emma asked.

I shook my head. "Nothing." I tried to brush past her, but she jumped in front of me. "Emma, move. I'm not in the mood. I'm tired. I'm pissed. And I'm going to bed."

"Take this the way it's intended. I don't want to see you hurt, so you can't keep doing this. Last time, it was a concussion and some bruises. Now, someone's shooting at you. Cops die all the time, Liv. It's not safe. You're smart and talented. You can do something else. Anything else. Why are you doing this?"

"Now you sound like my mom." That's when I realized what was going on. "Did she call you? Or did you call her?" I shoved my way past Emma, but she followed me into my bedroom. "You're supposed to be on my side. You're *my* friend."

"I am on your side. I am always on your side. That's why I had to say something."

"This is who I am. This is who I've always been. You've known it since the day you met me. I'm my father's daughter. And my mom will never understand what drove him or what drives me. I can't explain it." I gestured at the window. "But shit happens. It's happening right now. And someone has to do something about it. Women are being abducted. They're vanishing. We don't even know what's become of them, but we're trying to figure it out because if we don't more women will disappear. More people will be killed. More bad shit will happen." I took a shaky breath. "You're an ER nurse for christ's sake. You know what I'm talking about. You're doing something to help, and so am I."

Emma held up her hands. "You're right. But I lost two GSW victims tonight. One died before they wheeled him in, and the other died on the table. I don't want to see that happen to you. Do you hear me?" She sniffed and stormed out of the room.

I sighed. "Dammit." The bedroom door slammed. "Emma, I'm sorry." But I didn't know if she heard me.

Deciding to let her cool off, I took a shower and changed into pajama shorts and a t-shirt. Then I grabbed my gun off the counter, tucked it into my nightstand drawer, and went into the kitchen to make some hot cocoa. Emma might be a health food nut, but she wouldn't turn down hot cocoa and what was left of my mom's chocolate chip cookies.

I just put the mugs and cookies on a platter when my phone rang. I grabbed it, recognizing the precinct number. "Detective DeMarco." I turned off the stove.

"I thought you'd want to know, we just received confirmation of another abduction," Captain Grayson said.

"Shit. When? Where?"

"I'll text you the address. It just happened. 911 received a call. There was a witness this time. The vic matches the profile. Blonde, late teens. Units are rolling on the location. We issued a BOLO, and we've started a citywide manhunt. All off-duty personnel are back on duty. Since it's your case, you and Fennel are coordinating the search."

"Thanks for the heads-up. I'm on my way." I ran back into my room, changed clothes, grabbed my gear, and left a note for Emma. If she came out of her room, at least the cookies would soften the blow.

TWELVE

He cursed. He should have done it himself. He could have called Clarissa, made up some lie, and lured her to a secluded location. Instead, he asked a two-bit crook to do it for him. Another mistake. He couldn't afford any more mistakes. This had to stop.

He'd satisfy his Russian buyer and find some way to sell off the rest of the cargo. He always made it a point to avoid local buyers, but it'd be the fastest and easiest way to get rid of the evidence. With the authorities closing in, it was too hot to move the cargo overseas. Maybe, in a few months, things would die down, and he could start over.

She knocked, opening the door to his home office. He gave her a sad smile and held up a finger, indicating she give him a moment.

"I'll take care of it." He hung up the phone.

"Have you seen the news?" She grabbed the remote off the desk and flipped on the TV. "Another girl's been taken. I don't know what the world is coming to. How can this keep happening?"

"I don't know, dear." He wrapped his arms around

her and kissed her, but his eyes remained glued to the screen. "Do they have a suspect?"

"They gave a description of the car a few minutes ago." She pointed at the police sketch. "And they know what the girl looks like, but they don't know who she is. Isn't that terrible?"

"Terrible," he agreed, the anger boiling inside of him. The news showed some grainy footage and asked the public to notify the authorities if they spotted the car, the girl, or had any additional information to share. He kissed his wife's forehead. "I have to go to work. It's all-hands on deck. Everyone at the office is getting anxious. We have a deadline to meet."

She squeezed him tighter. "Promise me you'll be careful. Whoever's doing this is crazy. The news says he's armed and dangerous. And he could be anywhere."

"I'll be careful." He kissed the tip of her nose and smiled. "I love you."

"I love you too." She laughed. "How did I get so lucky to find such an amazing man when the world is full of psychos?"

*   *   *

"What do we know so far?"

Mac handed me a photograph. From the dark circles beneath her eyes and the slight tremor in her hands, I could tell she was exhausted. The only thing keeping her going was the energy drink she pounded. "Her name's Clarissa Berens. Nineteen years old. She lives on the street. No family. Few friends. She's in the system."

I read the file. Petty crimes. Larceny, mostly. Mac reached for her soda can, but I blocked her. "Go home, Laura."

"It's all-hands. You know that. I'm fine."

"You're not fine." I stared at her over the paperwork. "How many heart attacks were attributed to energy drinks last year?"

She held up her palms. She knew the answer. She had an uncanny knack for remembering macabre facts. I'd seen her spout out many impressive answers during trivia night at the bar across from the precinct.

"Okay. I get it." She backed away from her caffeine fix.

"Go home. Get some sleep." I pointed at the clock. "You've been working for almost twenty-four hours straight. No one will hold this against you."

Fennel came up beside us. "Do you want an officer to drive you home?"

"No, they need to continue the search." She looked at the two of us. "We'll get this guy. I can feel it."

"Sister Mary Catherine's on her way," Brad said. "She runs the church's homeless outreach program. She's the one who called in the tip and identified Clarissa from the sketch on the news."

"It's something." But it didn't feel like much. "What about the man who took her?" I had watched the footage several times since receiving the call. Our night began at the scene. We checked nearby traffic cams. We spoke to a few eyewitnesses, most of whom were also homeless, and canvassed the area. The description of the abductor and the details surrounding the incident were far from helpful. "Anything on him or the car?"

"Well, unless Keith Richardson is a zombie, he didn't take Clarissa."

"No shit."

"You're tired and bitchy."

I glared at my partner. "Can you blame me?" I crossed my arms over my chest and stared at the board. Clarissa's photo hung beside Jane Doe's. "I'm not imagining it. They look alike, right?"

"Blonde, young, thin." He shrugged. "Honestly, they look like jailbait."

"So you wouldn't try to pick either of them up in a bar?"

Brad spent a few moments thinking about the question. "Bar would indicate twenty-one and over, but as a cop, I know better. And as a man, I don't find either one attractive or sexy. They don't look old enough. They look too young. Like children. It's skeevy."

"Some men like that."

"Yeah, psychos and perverts. A lot of those guys are serving hard time."

I laughed sarcastically. "And yet, there are that many more still on the streets." I rolled my neck, listening to my vertebrae crack and pop, but I couldn't quite get rid of the tight pinch.

Fennel stepped behind me and dug his thumbs into the muscles at either side of my cervical spine. "You know we checked with the registered pedophiles in the area, but that was a bust."

"They aren't minors." I let my head hang, wincing when he found the knotted muscle just between my shoulder and neck.

"I know, but Clarissa looks fifteen. It didn't hurt to check." He waited for me to sigh before removing his hands. "Whoever took her didn't go far. We only spotted the car on a few traffic cams before it disappeared. We ran the plates, but it was reported stolen two weeks ago."

"Did uniforms question the owner?"

"Uh-huh. He even let them search his property. I don't think he's involved." Brad moved closer to the board. A large red circle on an area map indicated where all five abductions had taken place. He traced the car's route with a pen. "The women are being kept somewhere in the vicinity. They have to be. Or we would have seen the car."

"Do you think he'll kill her?" I asked. "Keith Richardson killed Jane Doe. We don't know about the others, Lyla, Abigail..."

"What did Richardson say to you?"

I shrugged. "*He* made me do it."

"*He.* Do you think *he* is the same guy who abducted Clarissa?"

"No."

Fennel stepped back and rested his hips on the desk. "Why not?"

"Assuming Richardson wasn't delusional, then the man who wanted Jane Doe dead wanted her dead for a reason. If killing was his primary goal, pleasure, power, whatever, he wouldn't have asked Richardson to do it. He would have done it himself. And Richardson wouldn't have been involved, so I think whoever forced Richardson to kill Doe probably got this other guy to take Clarissa."

"And we know Richardson lured Abigail Booker into his car, and she was never seen again. Maybe he did the same to Lyla James. Maybe Richardson was collecting women for some unknown bastard. And for some reason, the bastard wasn't pleased with Jane Doe, so he wanted Richardson to correct the mistake."

"And kill himself because of it?" It sounded crazy, but on no sleep and without any clear leads, I found some merit to Brad's theory.

"Maybe failure wasn't an option." My partner pointed at the grainy photo of a masked man tossing Clarissa into the trunk of the car. "We might be looking at Keith Richardson's replacement or the sick bastard who told Keith to off himself."

"Or an entirely unrelated case," Captain Grayson

said. A nun stood behind him, and he introduced us to Sister Mary Catherine.

We took her into the conference room and closed the door, thanking her for calling in the tip and stopping by to help. The church had some weird ideas when it came to protecting people, but we weren't asking a priest to break the sanctity of the confessional.

"I know Clarissa," the nun said. "I tried to encourage her to seek help. There are shelters and outreach programs. She didn't have to live on the streets. She didn't have to do anything alone. I wish she had listened."

"What else can you tell us about Clarissa? Did she have friends? Family? Anyone?" I asked.

"Clarissa's a runaway. I don't remember where she came from, but when she was sixteen, she left home. She wanted to be famous. A star. I don't think her home life was particularly nurturing."

"Abuse?" I asked.

The nun nodded. "She saved, stole, and borrowed to get here, but her reality didn't live up to her dreams. She scrapes together whatever she can and goes to every open call she can find. I tried to convince her to go back to school, but she doesn't listen. She begs on the street and sleeps at hostels and shelters. Most of the time, she goes hungry. A few weeks ago, she showed me her new headshots. No matter what life throws at her, she won't give up. I pray that's enough to get her through this."

"Headshots for what?" Brad asked.

"She wants to be a singer, but she hoped to get some advertising work until she's discovered. She heard models live in apartments and meet a lot of important people. For a girl who was lucky to find an empty metal cot most nights, the idea of work providing an apartment, even if it is overcrowded, must sound amazing."

"Do you recognize this man?" I held out a photo of Keith Richardson.

Sister Mary Catherine nodded. "I do. His name is Keith Boon."

Brad scoffed. "That son of a bitch." I nudged him with my elbow. "Sorry, Sister."

"I don't understand," she said.

I took the photo from her hand. "This man has been using several fictitious names, each an offshoot of a famous musician." I waved the thought away. "But that's not important. Can you describe your interactions with this man? When did you see him last? Did he know Clarissa?"

"The last time I saw Keith was Saturday. He works at the community center. He stops by the church once a week to collect donations. Clothes, blankets, that sort of thing. I find it hard to believe he's involved in a kidnapping. Keith is a good man. He does the Lord's work. I don't think he knows Clarissa. Why do you think he would abduct her?"

"We know he didn't take her." Brad spread out a few other photos. "Do you know any of these women?"

The nun took her time studying each photograph. "No, I don't." She put down the photos of Jane Doe, Abigail Booker, and Lyla James.

"Are you positive?" I asked.

"Yes. I do not know them."

"What about these women?" Brad laid out photos of the two missing hookers.

Mary Catherine glanced at them and nodded. "That's Yasmine and Tanya. I don't know if those are their real names. They're troubled." She looked up at my partner. "What is this about? I came here to help find Clarissa."

"Ma'am," Brad said, "these other women were also taken. We believe the same party is responsible. Anything you can tell us might be helpful."

She nodded, her focus returning to Keith Richardson. She poked at the glossy print. "And you think Keith's involved?"

"We're just covering our bases. What's the church's connection to the community center?" Brad asked.

"We work in concert with one another to help the community. Our neighborhood isn't bad. We don't have much in terms of violent crime or gang violence, but it's a poor area. We try to help our neighbors by making sure they have enough food to eat and a safe place to sleep."

"Did you ever send Clarissa to the community center?" Brad eyed me. He'd been convinced that was our connection, and the moment Sister Mary Catherine confirmed it with a nod, I saw the ah-ha look in his eyes. "May I ask why?"

"She cut her hand on a broken glass bottle. It got infected, so I sent her to the free clinic that's run by the community center." The nun looked at both of us. "Do you have any idea who took Clarissa or why he'd do such a thing?"

The police department had been trying to keep a lid on the recent abductions, but the nun might be able to help us. So I told her what was happening, and we spent the next hour taking notes on every detail and odd occurrence she could remember. At the end, we thanked her for her time, and a uniform escorted her downstairs.

I looked over the notes. "I'm not sure this helps."

"Probably not," Fennel admitted, "but let's just hope it didn't hurt." He knew we were on a clock. We just didn't know when time would run out. "We learned two valuable pieces of intel. One, we need to check the community center. It appears to be the root of all evil."

"And the other?"

"Clarissa Berens wanted to be a model."

"All right. Let's split up. We'll cover more ground that way. Modeling agency or community center?" I asked.

"I've been hot for the community center all along. That one's mine."

"Fine. I'll see if Rogers and Stein is finished remodeling yet. And if they aren't, maybe I'll offer to help."

THIRTEEN

"Detective DeMarco." I held out my badge. "I need to speak to someone in charge."

"Do you have an appointment?" the guy behind the desk asked. He could have been a model with his boyish good looks, stick thin physique, and the perfectly applied makeup he wore. He assessed me. "Is this about the uniform catalog? Decisions haven't been made yet, hun. But they'll call you."

I stared in utter disbelief. "Do you see this badge?" I practically shoved it in his face. "I'm not here about a catalog." I held out the court order. "I need to speak to someone in charge. So pick up that phone and get your boss out here."

"Fine," he huffed. He picked up the phone. "Mr. Crenshaw, a police detective is here. Should I contact legal?" He gave me a saccharine smile. "Sure. I'll see her in." He held the phony smile and stood up. "Mr. Crenshaw will see you now."

On the way down the hall, I peered into open doorways. The receptionist in the lobby didn't lie about the remodel. Plastic sheets and dust covered a lot of surfaces. A few workers were installing new lights in one of the rooms. Despite the mess, everything was crisp and sharp with modern accents. It looked like any other upscale office, even though this wasn't an upscale neighborhood.

"This is it." The receptionist stopped just outside the doorway.

"Thanks."

He gave me another fake smile, and I wondered if he was paid extra to be bitchy. He sashayed past and returned to the front desk. I knocked on the open door, probably out of habit, and stepped inside.

"Good morning." I placed my hand on my hip to emphasize the badge clipped to my belt. "I'm Detective DeMarco."

"Detective," Mr. Dale Crenshaw, head of Public Relations, stood, "is this about the noise? Or permits? I have the paperwork here." He pointed to a stack of files on his desk.

"No, sir. I just have a few questions about your staff." I wasn't sure how to categorize temps and models, but staff seemed broad enough to cover everything.

"Please," he gestured to the chair in front of his desk, "is this about the subpoena? We complied with the court order."

"And we appreciate it. I'm actually here to follow up. We have a few additional questions."

"We?"

"The police."

"Right." He leaned back in his chair and steepled his fingers before pointing at me. "Should I ask for my lawyer?" His eyes twinkled. Clearly, it was a joke, but I wasn't in a joking mood.

"Mr. Crenshaw, I need some information. I'm

aware Rogers and Stein hires temps."

"On occasion." He opened his drawer and pulled out a folder. "Here's our contract with A La Carte Hires. They provide assistants, receptionists, um," he flipped through the pages, "janitorial staff, and technical support as needed."

"Tell me about your photographers and recruiters."

"Recruiters?" He chuckled. "This isn't the army. We have a few talent scouts, but we don't recruit. We have in-house photographers, but we hire freelancers when necessary or when we're shooting off-site. Our talent scouts are full-time. We don't source that work out. It would lead to an unfair bias."

I examined the gold plaque behind his desk. It was an award for excellence in empowering women. "Are you aware of any problems?"

"What kinds of problems?"

"Complaints of sexual harassment, stalking, inappropriate workplace attitudes."

"I know we're living in a new age, Detective DeMarco. Is this about an allegation?"

"Just answer the question."

"Nothing has been brought to my attention. Rogers and Stein has a zero tolerance policy. Should an issue like that arise, we'd swiftly rectify it."

"Tell me about the audition process."

He nearly laughed. "Are you hoping to moonlight?"

"Sir," I said sternly, "please humor me."

"Depending on the ad campaign, we might issue a casting call if we don't have a person who fits our needs. Other agencies are made aware. They'll send us the information on their clients. We review those files. If we believe someone is a match, we'll call them in. We might take a few shots to send to our client. That's about it."

"Do you ever have open calls?"

"Sometimes." He saw where the conversation was heading and volunteered the information. "We block out a few hours. People come in with their headshots and CVs. A team reviews the paperwork immediately. If we like what we see, we tell them to wait. If we don't, we send them home. The ones who are asked to wait are photographed and evaluated. Then we take it from there."

"What happens to the personal information you collect?"

"It gets destroyed. Rogers and Stein takes privacy rights very seriously." Tired of answering questions, Crenshaw asked, "What is this about?"

"Rogers and Stein was mentioned during the course of an investigation. I just have to dot the 'I's and cross the 'T's." Reaching into my inner jacket pocket, I removed a few photographs. "Do you recognize any of these people?"

While he examined the photographs, I watched him. He studied the photos of Abigail Booker and Keith Richardson without batting an eye. "I don't believe so."

"Have you had any open calls for young, blonde women recently?"

"I'm not in charge of that. Give me a minute. I'll find out." He left his office, and I glanced back at the door.

Conducting a search without a warrant was illegal, but anything in plain sight was fair game. The documents on his desk were work related, containing details on severance packages, performance reviews, and employee grievances. I scanned the grievances, but they were mostly missed pay or incorrect hours. Like Crenshaw said, no one had filed a sexual harassment complaint or anything worse. And if they did, he didn't keep it on his desk. The walls were covered in images from Rogers and Stein's most successful modeling campaigns. Their models had been used to advertise some high-end timepieces, sunglasses, and fashion. Turning, I noticed the label on the jacket hanging behind the door. Hearing footsteps approaching, I moved to the window and stared outside.

"It's terrible, isn't it?"

"What?" I asked, spinning.

"The view. It's hideous." He held out a sheet of paper. "That's the information we sent to the agencies. According to HR, they also posted the call on our website."

I read the date. Two weeks ago, Rogers and Stein had been swarming with perky, young blondes. "How much do these gigs pay? Do the models get room and board?"

"It varies. The biggest perk is getting to keep the samples left behind. Suits, handbags, sunglasses."

"Does that happen every time?" Clarissa might have wanted the gig just to pawn the high-end items.

"It depends on the advertiser. We have a closet in back where we keep the gear. It's a nice reward for a job well done."

"And the rumored model apartments? Are those just rumors?"

"No, but not every model stays in one of our apartments. Those are usually reserved for runway, specific locales, fashion week. Special circumstances."

"I see."

"Detective, I have work to do. Is there anything else?"

"Just one more thing. Do you know if these women showed up for that audition?" I handed him photographs of Jane Doe and Clarissa Berens.

He looked at the women, a slight furrow to his

brow. "Do you know their names?" He held out the photo of Clarissa. "She looks familiar, like I just saw her."

"Were you at the casting call?"

"No."

"We don't have an ID on that one." I pointed to Jane Doe. "But the other is Clarissa Berens."

"Huh." He retook his seat and typed her name into an internet search. "She was abducted last night. The news has been running her name and picture all morning. That's why you're here. But you requested our files before..." He looked at the other photo. "Ms. Berens wasn't the first, was she?"

"No. Where were you when Rogers and Stein held the casting call?"

"I was at a friend's wedding." He must have seen the suspicious look on my face. "I'll get you names."

"Thanks."

He wrote down a dozen names and corresponding phone numbers and handed me the sheet of paper. "Ms. Berens doesn't work for us. We don't have her information on file. I don't know if she was here that day or not. I'm sorry I can't be more helpful."

I placed my card on his desk. "In case you think of something, don't hesitate."

"I won't."

Before leaving, I spoke to several other Rogers and Stein employees, but no one recognized any of the women or Keith Richardson. Perhaps they were lying, but I didn't have hard proof any of the victims stepped foot inside the office. Everything was hearsay and speculation. However, I didn't believe a nun would lie. Clarissa wanted to be a model. I just didn't know if that meant she went to an open call at Rogers and Stein or she tried her luck someplace else.

On my way back to the station, I couldn't help but

think of everything and nothing. I sent Mac home because she was exhausted, but Fennel and I had been at this almost as long. Nothing was making sense, but that might have been because I couldn't think straight. After stopping at a juice bar and picking up two green smoothies, I returned to work. Hopefully, Brad was having better luck.

"DeMarco," the desk sergeant said, "FBI Agent Peters is here to see you. I put him in one of the empty interrogation rooms. Thought you might like some privacy."

"Are you getting a kick out of that?"

"Whatever do you mean?" he asked innocently.

"Play nice," I warned. "We need Peters' help."

I dropped the smoothies off and opened the door to interrogation. Peters stood in the corner, his hands in his pockets. He nodded at a file on the table.

"Thought I should drop that off. I'm sorry, Detective. I wish I had better news."

I picked up the file and rested my hips on the table. The DNA they recovered from the charred bones matched the DNA the ME's office had on record for Jane Doe and Keith Richardson.

"How did this happen?" I asked.

Peters sighed. "I wish I knew. We've gone over everything. The FBI offices are supposed to be secure, especially the motor pool and garage. The only people with access are government agents."

"Someone in your office is dirty. That's what I'm hearing."

"We checked the records. Your team checked our records. The two imposters gained access to the garage using an ID. It was fake. Andrew Savage. That's the name on the badge they used, but we don't have any agents named Andrew Savage."

"Shouldn't someone have checked before giving

him keys to a van?"

"I don't know. When you access the evidence locker, do they run your badge number and ID to make sure you're who you claim to be?"

"Point taken."

Peters' phone rang, and he glanced at the display before hitting ignore. "I just thought you'd like to know. According to the police techs I spoke to, these men, Andrew Savage and his partner or whatever aliases they are using now, used the same tactics to get into the ME's office and cart off the bodies. That's a lot of extra work to go through just to destroy evidence. They wouldn't have needed an FBI van or FBI credentials to steal some bodies. And impersonating a federal agent is a serious crime to add to their growing list of felonies, so why did they go to that much trouble?"

"That's a good question." Unfortunately, I didn't have an answer.

"Just something to think about." His phone rang again. "Excuse me." He hit answer. "Hi, honey. Is everything okay?"

While he spoke on the phone, I read the reports and studied the stills taken from the security footage. The imposters avoided the cameras. They were careful. They knew the layout of the federal building. They must have been inside at some point prior to stealing the van. I glanced at Peters, wondering if the imposters were actual FBI agents pretending to be different FBI agents.

"I will. Love you, too." He hung up. "Sorry about that. My wife worries."

"Makes sense." I flipped to the last two pages. "According to this, the imposters split up at the body dump. One stayed behind to destroy the remains while the other returned the van."

"Yes. The thin one dropped off the van and walked out the side exit. He kept his head down. We have a team hoping to pull a reflection off a window or shiny surface, but so far, we've had no luck."

"What about the second one? How did he elude us?"

"Nearby security cameras caught a man matching his description getting into a car. It's the same car used in Clarissa Berens' abduction, but it's not the same guy who abducted her. The FBI imposter has a heavier build than the man who snatched Clarissa, but I'm sure the same people are responsible for the stolen bodies and the kidnapping. Director Kendall has made it clear we are at your disposal. Let me know what we can do to help."

"We need to find the car."

Peters nodded. "We're on it."

FOURTEEN

Peters raised some very good questions. Why would anyone go to the trouble of stealing an FBI van just to take two bodies from the morgue? And that's when I realized the imposters feared their credentials wouldn't hold up under scrutiny. The cheap suits and sunglasses would only go so far, and unlike the FBI motor pool which expected to see FBI agents come and go, the ME's office would have wanted the proper paperwork before handing over evidence. And the imposters couldn't provide it. They didn't have valid case numbers, and the ME's office would have discovered it the moment they called for verification. The van was meant to sell their cover. That had to be the only reason they'd go to that much trouble. They must have believed they wouldn't get caught. Maybe they even thought the van would cover their tracks entirely by convincing the PD that the FBI had taken over the case. After all, under any other circumstances, identifying a killer and finding evidence of his kill was enough to close a case and end the investigation. And with the ME's backlog, no one would have missed the bodies. We shouldn't have been the wiser.

"What's this?" Brad jiggled the cup on his desk.

"Breakfast."

Fennel took a sip and smacked his lips. "Pineapple, banana, and something else."

"Mango."

"Thanks, Liv. You're the best. I take back all the terrible things I said about you."

I narrowed my eyes at him. "So, how'd it go?"

"I had to call for a court order. We won't know more until it gets served." He took another sip from the cup and tapped on his desk. "The ink should be drying as we speak."

"You found something?"

"I spoke to David Hennen again. He doesn't just run the AA meeting. He manages the community center's various programs. He wasn't pleased about our deception."

"He can get over it."

"Anyway, he identified Keith Richardson as Tobias Keith. Keith volunteered and worked at the information desk. His duties included deliveries and pick-ups, answering questions, and directing walk-ins wherever they needed to go."

"That sounds risky since the church knew him as Keith Boon."

"I guess Sister Mary Catherine and David Hennen don't travel in the same circles."

"Did Keith have access to private information?"

"He might have. He collected paperwork for the free clinic since it's paid for by the community center. It's in a separate building, an annex, as they call it, but it's only two doors over. And according to David, Keith ran whatever errands anyone needed. He also coached some of the rec center's youth leagues. Basketball, volleyball, and," Brad squinted, trying to recall the other one, "I want to say badminton. But to play on a team, forms had to be filled out. Next of kin, permission slips, that sort of thing."

"For a killer, Keith was a real nice guy," I said sarcastically.

"Oh, yeah. He was a peach." Fennel slurped down more of his smoothie. "The youth leagues covered anyone twenty-one and younger. So maybe Abigail or Lyla participated at some point. I still think the community center is key to figuring out why these women were targeted."

"That doesn't explain the court order for the medical records."

"I'm getting to that." Fennel put down his cup. "David said Yasmine, Tanya, and several other working girls used the clinic when necessary. We know Lyla hung posters for the community theater on the board, and the Sister told us she sent Clarissa to get her hand examined. The only two we haven't placed at the community center are Jane Doe and Abigail Booker. But it looks promising. I think we found this predator's hunting grounds."

I held up my cup. "Cheers."

Brad bumped his cup with mine. "We need coffee."

Or sleep, I thought. But neither of us would voice it with Clarissa missing. She'd been taken eight hours ago. "We need to find the car. We need to find the woman. The longer she's gone, the harder it will be to track her."

"I know, and she might be able to lead us to the others."

I updated Brad on the intel Agent Peters gave us. "Every available police officer and FBI agent is looking for the car and Clarissa. The car used in

Clarissa's abduction was originally located at the dump site. That was Hardy's means of escape."

"And we know it was reported stolen two weeks prior to that. Hardy, he's the fat one, right? Hardy must have stolen it and stashed it there for when he needed it."

"That means they've been planning this a long time." I didn't like the thoughts going through my mind. "I know officers have already canvassed the area, but I can't stay here. I have to do something."

"Go," Fennel said. "I'll wait for the records. Just be careful, Liv."

But I didn't go. Instead, I froze in front of the board. The red circle and Xs on the area map caught my eye. "Actually, let's rework this." I took the map down. "Everything we need is here. We're just not seeing it." I didn't know if that was true, but I didn't know where else to look. I needed the answers to be here. Clarissa and the other women needed them to be here.

"I'll pull traffic cam footage." Fennel entered a few commands into the computer.

The car used in Clarissa's abduction had been parked behind the warehouse. Hardy stayed behind to make sure the bodies burned. After he was done, he exited through the back, peeled a tarp off the car, and drove away.

I watched the footage again. I hadn't seen it before because we didn't know where to look, but that changed thanks to Agent Peters. I watched the bastard pull open the door and hotwire the car.

"The starter's busted," Fennel noted.

"Yeah, but that didn't stop him from eventually getting it to go." The car drove off the screen. "Follow that car."

"Yeah, I'm trying." Fennel worked the computer,

bringing up dozens of little squares with relevant traffic cam footage. We watched the car leave the warehouse district, take some side streets, double back, turn, and vanish. "Hang on." He paused the footage and marked the route on the map. "Several hours later, we pick up the car again here." He pointed to a spot fairly close. "The driver's different. See." He pointed to an image of a much thinner man. He left the engine running, got out of the car, jogged up beside Clarissa, and nabbed her off the street.

"He must have been following her. She wasn't stationary. Why don't we have any other footage of the car? Where are our blind spots?"

Brad brought up a map marked with traffic cam locations and reached for a pen. "Hardy must have disappeared somewhere in here. And this other guy picked up the car and stayed off our radar."

I looked at the four square blocks and checked the camera locations. "What about here and here?"

"No cameras."

I grabbed Jane Doe's file off my desk. "She was found here. No area footage showing how she got there."

"That's reasonably close. I'd say it's in the same vicinity."

"It's like a big blackhole in the middle of our investigation." I didn't like the blind spots. Bad things happened in those areas. Women were killed. Accomplices vanished. Several office buildings were on the fringe of the blackout zone, including the building which housed Rogers and Stein. At the far right corner of the blackout zone was the community center, and on the other end was the Monthly Stay Condos. "Somewhere in here are our body snatchers and the missing women."

Fennel whistled. "You know patrols have been all

over this place. No one's seen or heard anything. We haven't even spotted the car, and according to the traffic cams, it drove back into the blind spot and never reappeared."

"Where do you think they are?"

Brad clicked a few more keys. "The city has hundreds of cameras, but a lot of places aren't covered. It's conceivable they found a way out."

"With the entire city on alert? I doubt it. They'd have to dump the car and get a new one. But where did they hide the first one?"

While Fennel mapped out every street and alleyway that could be used to aid in their escape, I checked for garages and storage sites, anything big enough to stash a car. "Kincaid knows how to make cars disappear."

Brad looked up, concern in his eyes. "Axel Kincaid?"

"Yeah."

"It's your dime, Liv." Fennel went back to the computer, glancing up surreptitiously to see if I was going to make the call.

It hadn't been that long since I infiltrated Kincaid's club in the hopes of building a case against the car thief turned legitimate businessman. We didn't exactly part on the best of terms. Although, for a suspected criminal, Axel was far more cordial than most men I arrested. Still, asking for his help would be like throwing lit matches at a kerosene tank. Eventually, it would blow up in my face.

The phone rang, and Fennel grabbed it. He listened for several moments. "How narrow?" He put it on speaker.

"Medical privacy rights are highly guarded. The judge doesn't see any reason why you'd need access to them," ADA Winters said.

"We don't. I just need to know if the missing women went to the clinic or used other services provided by the community center."

"That I can do. The clinic will be able to tell you yes or no, but that's the end of it."

"Fine by me. Thanks." Brad picked up the receiver and put it down. "I'll run with this. Do you want to continue the search for the car?"

"Might as well." I stifled a yawn. "Good luck."

FIFTEEN

It must have been exhaustion or desperation. Standing outside of Spark went against my better judgment. In the middle of the day, the nightclub didn't look like much, but it was after three. Axel Kincaid should be inside, prepping for the night to come.

The front door was locked, and I pressed the intercom button. A moment later, a familiar voice asked what I wanted.

"Hey, Rick. It's Liv. Is Mr. Kincaid in?"

"I'll check."

Rick didn't have to check. Kincaid was there. If he wasn't, Rick wouldn't be working the front door. What Rick had to check was whether Axel was willing to speak to me. I didn't hold my breath. When this turned out to be a pointless endeavor, I planned to head home and sleep for a few hours. Captain Grayson ordered me to do so and vowed to send Fennel home just as soon as he got back to the station. The captain didn't expect us to continue functioning when we were coming up on the thirty-six hour mark. Clarissa was gone, and at this point, two more detectives wouldn't make a huge difference to the ongoing search efforts.

The door opened, and Kincaid stood in front of me in a wrinkled, white dress shirt and suit pants. No tie. No jacket. His hair was mussed, and I wondered if he just left a woman upstairs in his loft.

"Detective," his tone matched the ice blue of his eyes, "I knew we'd cross paths again. What crime are you hoping to pin on me this time?"

"None." I regretted knocking almost as much as the next words out of my mouth. "I need your help."

"I'm intrigued." He leaned against the doorjamb, refusing to invite me inside.

"I need to know how to make a car vanish."

He snickered. "I wouldn't know."

"Have you seen the news? A woman was taken. They've been playing the security footage on a loop. It aired at noon."

"I wasn't awake."

"Well, it was on at six and throughout the night, ever since it happened. Please, Axel, I just need to know where to look."

"You searched traffic cam footage?"

I nodded.

"But you lost sight of it?"

"Yeah."

"Garages, parking and otherwise. Warehouses. Storage rentals. Parking lots with obstructed views. Beneath overpasses."

"We checked them all."

"With the right team and equipment, the plates could be changed and the car repainted in less than two minutes. Are you sure it isn't hiding in plain sight?"

"Not that we've seen."

He reached for the door. "I haven't heard anything, Detective. I'll let you know if I do."

"It's not high-end. I doubt you'd hear about it."

"You'd be surprised." For the briefest moment, concern flicked across his face. "You look like shit. Get some rest." And he shut the door.

"Thanks a lot." I trudged back to my car. Kincaid didn't tell me anything I didn't already know. On my drive home, I wondered why I even bothered. "You know why," I said aloud as I went up the steps. "You have to find her. You have to find them. So pull it together, DeMarco." Finished with my pep talk, I unlocked the door.

The cookies remained on the counter, and the pot was still on the stove. Obviously, Emma was still mad. I tossed the water in the sink, left the pot in the drain, and collapsed on the bed.

For a few short hours, there was nothingness. But my subconscious mind didn't allow the reprieve to last long. While I slept, it gnawed on everything we'd learned and Kincaid's words. Blinking open my eyes, I rolled over and glanced at the clock. It was just after seven. I hadn't even changed out of my clothes. My badge was still hooked on my belt. At least I had the foresight to remove my firearm and shoes.

"Hiding in plain sight," I mumbled. Getting up, I brushed my teeth, ran a comb through my hair, and checked for messages. Fennel didn't call, and neither did the station, which meant we hadn't found anything. "Dammit."

Taking a seat at the kitchen counter, I chomped on a stale cookie and stared out the window. We knew the make and model of the car. Those things couldn't be changed, but everything else could.

I packed up the rest of the cookies and grabbed my keys. We were missing something. Clarissa had been taken nineteen hours ago. Based on statistics, the first twenty-four were crucial. We had five hours to find her before our chances substantially diminished. And then she'd just be another photo hanging on the board beside the others. I couldn't let that happen. I just didn't know how to stop it.

I'd been driving around for almost two hours when Fennel called. He couldn't sleep either. We had to find Clarissa. We agreed to meet up, and I parked my car on the top level of the garage. Ever since I left the apartment, I'd been checking every possible location Kincaid mentioned. Every other law enforcement officer had already done it, but maybe Axel was right. Maybe they repainted the car and ditched the plates. Hell, they might have re-etched the VIN.

The police had gone door to door to every chop shop and garage in search of the vehicle used in the abduction, but it was nowhere to be found. Every officer and detective I knew had gone to their CIs, hoping to get some tidbit of information, but those results had been just as fruitless. That left two possibilities. It was hidden on private property, or it was here. Somewhere.

I had physically checked the first four levels of the garage by the time Brad arrived. The unmarked cruiser stopped beside me, and he rolled down the window. "Hey, Liv, where did you park?"

"Top level."

"Okay. I'll be down in a sec." He drove past while I finished checking the row of vehicles and moved around the corner to the next set. The elevator dinged, and my partner stepped out. He rubbed at the scruff on his jaw. "Didn't Grayson tell you to take the rest of the night?"

"I couldn't sleep."

"Me neither."

While we continued to search the rows of vehicles, Fennel updated me on his findings. Yasmine, Tanya, and Clarissa had visited the free clinic in the last six weeks. Based on our timeline, Yasmine's visit occurred only a day or two before her disappearance. And Lyla volunteered at the community center to help with an acting class they offered the previous month.

"What about Abigail and Jane Doe?"

"I showed Jane Doe's photo around, but no one's talking. Every worker and volunteer directed me back to David. I'm not sure if they're afraid of him or they respect him, but he gives me bad vibes."

"Even in the AA meeting?"

"Especially in the AA meeting. Didn't he seem fake to you? Like he was trying too hard or," Brad shook his head, hoping to knock the thought loose, "he wanted to lord his sobriety over them or something. I don't know."

"I guess." I tried to think back, but I'd been more focused on remembering faces and learning names than listening to what David had to say.

"I don't know, but I don't trust him. I think he knows more than he's letting on. Units are sitting on the community center, and a secondary team has orders to shadow David. So we'll see what happens. The community center doesn't have any record of Abigail Booker. We still don't know where she crossed paths with Keith, but we know she did, not that it even matters anymore."

"Don't say that." I bumped against his shoulder. "Have we looked into Nicky? Could she be involved?"

"She doesn't have a record, but it's hard to clear her under the circumstances."

"Let's put a surveillance team on her too, just in case."

"Yeah, okay." Brad made the request since he had a

better relationship with dispatch, and I finished my examination of the parked cars. "Are you going to tell me what you're hoping to find?"

"I went to see Axel Kincaid. Since he's a car thief, he should know how to hide a car. He suggested the car might have been repainted and the plates exchanged. So I'm checking every car that matches the make and model." I sighed. "I don't know what else to do."

We left the garage and continued our search. Eventually, it led to the Monthly Stay Condos. A blue four-door sat in the middle of a row of cars. It was the same make and model as the one used in Clarissa's abduction. I peered into the windows, but I couldn't see anything inside. Brad checked the VIN in the windshield, but it didn't match the one reported stolen.

"That's the easiest one to change," I said. VINs were listed in three separate locations on a car – the dash, the inside of the door, and the rear of the frame.

Taking off his jacket, Brad spread it out on the ground and laid on top of it. With his flashlight in hand, he checked the frame. "It's corroded. I can't make it out."

"Do you think that was intentional?"

"I can't tell." Brad stood, knocked the dirt off his jacket, and put it back on. "Motels register guest vehicles, right? Why don't we run the plate against the VIN and go inside and get the owner's name and see if it matches? That'd be easiest."

"Okay."

I surveyed the area. Based on the interior lights, it appeared more than half the rooms were currently occupied. I wondered if the women I encountered last time were still staying here. I had no reason to knock, but I was starting to get a bad feeling. I reached for my phone but didn't move from the spot.

"Are you coming, Liv?"

"In a minute. I just want to check on something out here first."

"Do you need backup?"

"No, it might be best if we maintain some distance."

"What are you planning?"

"I'm not sure yet."

"Let me know when you figure it out, preferably before you do something asinine."

I laughed. "Me?"

He gave me an all-too familiar look.

"I'll think about it." Without waiting for Brad's sarcastic reply, I headed in the direction of the first floor vending machines.

The motel had a collection of condos. The main building had interior corridors, but the first floor condos that faced the parking lot had exterior access. I passed the vending machine and lingered outside the door. No light came from within, and I didn't hear any sounds. Perhaps the women were out for the evening, or they checked out of the motel.

The crying was the only thing that made me suspicious, but women crying wasn't a rare occurrence. The world was hard. People cried. Life went on. My gaze went back to the car, and I dialed the station and waited for an answer to the car owner's identity. The VIN matched the plate, which was registered to a Nathan Lence.

"Anything else, Detective?"

"Probably not, but if that changes, I'll get back to you." More than likely, the guest registry would have a listing for Nathan Lence and this would turn into yet another dead end. As I approached the lobby, I checked the time. We had less than two hours to find

Clarissa, and the last bit of hope fizzled out of me.

We didn't know why women were being taken, but our best guess was human trafficking. Without additional bodies turning up, it made the most sense. The victims weren't likely to be missed. But someone missed Abigail, and enough people realized Lyla was gone to take notice. The real kicker was Clarissa Berens' abduction.

Now we were on to them. If this was a human trafficking ring, they'd scatter. And I didn't think we had enough to find them. Our only lead jumped off the roof and had his remains stolen. Once more, I found myself dwelling on all the ways this case had gone awry. Keith Richardson's real identity would cinch the case. I didn't know how or why, but I knew it would. We needed a miracle.

SIXTEEN

"Did he view the merchandise?" he asked. The police were desperately searching for Clarissa Berens. They wouldn't leave any rock or stone unturned. He had to unload her as soon as possible. The Russian said he wanted the blonde. Hopefully, he accepted delivery that way Clarissa would no longer be his problem.

"He wasn't interested. There's too much heat on the girl. He didn't want to take the risk."

"Did he take any of the others?"

"Three."

"Shit," he cursed, "only three."

"What do you want me to do with the rest, boss?"

"Move them to the auction site. They've seen too much. They know too much. We need to get rid of them one way or the other. If the police get their hands on them, we're fucked."

"And the ones in the stable?"

He remained in his car and watched the scene unfold from his windshield. "I'll speak to Ivan. Ingrid was clever and escaped, but the rest don't seem to realize the reality of their situation. I'd like to keep it that way. Since they don't know their real purpose, we should keep up the charade for now. Releasing them all at once will make the girls suspicious. So we'll keep them a while longer and slowly trickle their release. They'll just think they weren't good enough to be selected. They'll never know how lucky they were."

"What do you want me to do with Clarissa?"

"Is she still at the house?"

"Yes."

He hunkered down farther in his seat and watched the two police detectives scout the motel parking lot. They shouldn't be here. They shouldn't be this close. *Keith, you bastard*, he thought. If they discovered his stable, he'd have to kill them all. It would be a waste of money, time, and human life. "Move Clarissa first. And use a different car. The police are looking for that vehicle. Leave it at the house. I'll send a team to scrap it. How's security? Did the Russian withdraw his men?"

"No. Dmitri and Yuri are keeping watch on the house."

"Okay. Tell them to expect my team. In the meantime, move those girls to the auction site. And do it one at a time. Make sure you aren't tailed. The police are everywhere."

"Yes, sir."

*　　*　　*

"Nathan Lence," Brad said.

"That's the same name on the vehicle registration." I rubbed my face. "We're not going to find her in time."

Fennel led the way back to the cars. "Let's go back to the station and analyze the intel."

"Yeah, okay." Since we didn't find the car or the woman, the hopelessness and depression seeped into my soul. Everything we did was an utter waste.

Fennel leafed through the intel we gathered, checked statements, and cross-referenced details to see if anyone lied or if the overlap might lead us in the right direction. I focused my efforts on finding out who could orchestrate this. We knew Keith must have identified the targets. Since he was the last person seen with Abigail, he probably abducted her, possibly Lyla too. And he killed Jane Doe. But some other man was pulling the strings, and he had an entire team working for him.

I stared at the sketches of the two FBI impersonators. They gained access to the FBI garage, the ME's office, and who knows what else. And a third man abducted Clarissa Berens off the street. That made five suspects involved in these abductions. The car used in the abduction remained MIA, and the FBI van had been scrubbed clean.

Maybe the techs found something at the ME's office. Leaving my desk, I went to check on the progress they made. Even though I sent Mac home several hours earlier, she left the computer running and her notes out. Another member of cyber division picked up the slack.

It didn't take long to locate the report. The ME's internal cameras had been remotely hacked. That's how the men knew when it was safe to enter. They probably hadn't counted on Dr. Emerson interrupting their getaway, but it didn't take much to convince the doc to let them leave.

"Is anyone really that gullible?" I asked, returning to my desk. "The bodies went missing. The imposters were aware of the security measures and knew how to circumvent them. It could be an inside job."

"You think Doc Emerson's involved?" Brad considered the possibility. "He would know what types of crimes and victims get the least amount of attention. But what's his endgame? Murder? Human trafficking? We've been to his house. It's just him, his wife, and their two cats. I'm guessing what we see is what we get."

"It can't hurt to check." Since he was a government employee, accessing Emerson's records wasn't too difficult. Emerson was sitting on a small fortune. He had no reason to moonlight, and I didn't see any strange fluctuations in his financials. His wife was a biology professor at the same university Lyla James attended, but that was the only connection I could find between the ME and our missing women. As far as I could tell, he didn't have much incentive to kidnap young women, unless he was a sadistic pervert, which was entirely possible.

Disgusted, I turned back to the board. Since I couldn't locate Clarissa, I had to identify the man responsible. The failure continued to eat away at me. We had dozens of units searching the city for the car and the woman. How could we still be in the dark?

My phone rang, and I grabbed it.

"The car's on Tremont. Hurry."

"Who is this?" I asked, but the caller hung up. "I need to know who just phoned my desk." I looked around the room. A couple of uniforms stared at me. "Get on it. Now."

"What's up?" Fennel asked.

"The car's on Tremont. Let's move."

I didn't know who the caller was, but I knew the tip was legit. We raced to the location. No sirens. No lights. We didn't want to scare off the kidnapper. Two backup units lingered nearby, ready to jump in or set up a perimeter.

"There." I pointed, and Brad parked at an angle behind the sedan. The plates matched the stolen vehicle. I threw open the door and aimed at the car. Brad and I circled from opposite sides. I peered in the rear window, then the front. "Clear."

With gloved hands, Fennel opened the driver's door and hit the trunk release. "DeMarco?"

"She's not here." I holstered my weapon. "Fuck."

The car had been left in a private driveway, partially concealed by a privacy fence and some trashcans. I didn't want to think about how many units drove past and never noticed it. Fennel moved to the front of the car and placed his hand on the hood.

"It's warm."

That got my attention, and I reached for my gun. Brad used hand signals, and we split up to scout the property. For the hood to be warm, the car couldn't have been here that long. The tipster must have followed it here, or the kidnapper called to gloat. Either way, I didn't care. I just hoped Clarissa was close.

I moved to the front door while Brad went around back. The door was locked, and I checked the windows. But there was no way to see inside.

"Liv," Fennel whispered, gesturing for me to join him.

I crept away from the door and followed my partner around the side of the house. Leaving the front door unguarded wasn't wise, but it was just the two of us for now.

"Upstairs." He pointed to a window.

I looked up at the second floor. The blinds gently swayed back and forth, but I didn't see anyone. With the way the windows were covered, we couldn't get eyes inside. I kept watch on the house while he checked the tool shed at the end of the property. The door opened, but no one was inside.

"Clear," he whispered, returning to our position.

Fennel and I ran at a crouch, keeping low and moving from cover to cover. A branch snagged my hair, so I tucked my ponytail into the back of my collar as I maneuvered through the bushes. At the back door, Brad stopped, listening for sounds coming from inside.

He tried the knob, but the place was locked up tight. Still, for the engine to be warm, someone had to be here. "I don't hear anything." He moved to a window and peered in. Shaking his head, he checked the other window before returning to the back door. "Maybe he ditched the car and took off in another vehicle. We should wait for backup. Go cover the front."

But before I could move an inch, a muffled scream came from inside the house. I reached for the radio, advising the incoming units we were entering the house from the rear and they needed to secure the front. They'd be here in a minute, but the woman screaming might not have that long.

Fennel took a step back and kicked in the door. He went in high and to the right. I followed low and to the left. The rear door opened into a narrow hallway. The first room we came to was the laundry room. It was empty.

Fennel moved deeper into the house. At the end of the hallway, he pressed his back against the wall and peered around the corner. When he didn't spot anyone, he spun into the living room, letting the barrel of his Glock lead the way. I branched out in the opposite direction.

Another scream sounded, but I couldn't determine where it came from. I burst into the bedroom, announcing myself as I entered, but the room was empty. Where was she?

A creak from above halted us in our tracks. "Stairs," Fennel called, moving through the main room and heading for the staircase.

"Right behind you." I finished my check of the bedroom and followed him to the stairs. We had no idea how many hostiles were inside, but we knew someone was upstairs.

The front door slammed inward, and Fennel and I flew apart like shrapnel, seeking cover. Three uniformed officers entered the house while the third stowed the ram. I held up my badge and informed them of the situation.

A second staircase leading down caught my eye. She could be in the basement. The six of us split up. Two uniforms took the staircase down. The other police officer and his partner guarded the main level, ensuring no one escaped through the front or back.

I tapped Brad on the shoulder, and he led the way up the steps. The first shot was so loud everything that followed was almost muted. Three more shots went off in rapid succession. One of them tore into the wall above my head, and I hit the ground. I aimed at the source of the barrage, but from this angle, I couldn't see anyone. The bastard had to be hiding inside the room at the top of the steps.

"Police, drop your weapons," Fennel announced. Gunfire reverberated throughout the house, and sounds of a scuffle grew louder. We weren't the only ones under fire.

In response, more bullets flew our way. We needed to get off the stairs. Go up or retreat? Those were our two options. A bullet from below splintered the railing, and I jumped back. Down was no longer viable.

"Are you hit?" Fennel asked.

"No. I'm good." I keyed my radio. "Shots fired at police. All available units, please respond."

"Cover me." Fennel dashed up the remaining steps.

When he made it to the top, he ducked against the wall. He signaled to me, and I ran up the stairs, keeping my head down and my gun aimed. I darted across the open doorway, and another two shots narrowly missed me.

"Police," I bellowed. "We have you surrounded. Toss out your weapons, and come out with your hands up."

In response, the doorframe splintered from a shotgun blast, and I tucked myself into the corner. So much for playing nice.

"Where's the rest of our backup?" Fennel muttered, seeing them pinned down below us.

I gestured for Brad to wait, and I reached for one of the glass sconces that dotted the hallway. I lifted it off the lightbulb and forced my breathing to slow. "Ready?"

Fennel nodded, and I tossed the glass fixture into the room. The shooter spun and fired. My partner darted into the room and tackled the man.

"Watch out!" The warning came from below.

I didn't even have time to process what it meant before a spray of bullets peppered the wall. I dove into the corner and dropped to my belly. The gunfire abated, but a fight broke out downstairs. Glass shattered, and the walls shook as screams and growls replaced the deafening weapons' discharge.

"Offender down," the officer below announced.

Pushing to my feet, I burst into the bedroom after my partner. Fennel had wrestled the shotgun away from the shooter, but the man had my partner in a headlock.

"Let him go," I snarled.

The abrupt command caused the attacker to have a momentary lapse, and Fennel slammed him backward into a wall. The offender's grip loosened, and Brad elbowed him in the jaw, turning and swinging with a right hook followed closely by a left jab. The guy crumpled to the ground, and Fennel reached for his cuffs. The wall next to me was riddled with bullet holes, but they weren't from a shotgun. I couldn't remember how many shots I heard, but there had to be another weapon, possibly another shooter.

"Are you okay?" I asked.

Fennel nodded and cuffed the prick. "Downstairs?"

"I don't know."

"We need to wrap this up and get down there."

While Fennel frisked the suspect, I inched forward to check the rest of the room. We were inside the master bedroom. I eyed the three closed doors. With my gun in hand, I carefully threw open the first one. It was a walk-in closet. I peered inside, but it was clear.

I was just reaching for the next door handle when the door flew open with enough force to knock the gun from my hands. A large, burly man launched himself at me. The guy looked like a steroid-addled linebacker due to his sheer bulk and height. I dove for my gun, but it was too late. He was already on top of me.

He batted the gun away before I could reach it, wrapped his hands around my neck, and lifted me off the ground. I struggled and kicked, but his grip only tightened. I tried to wrap my legs around him, needing the leverage, but he kept me at arms' length.

"Fennel," I sputtered. I kicked again, hoping to loosen the offender's grip by breaking his balls. Unfortunately, the guy turned to the side, making my kick ineffectual. My foot glanced off his thigh, and he continued to hold firm.

I couldn't breathe. My head started to swim. "Son

of a bitch." I kicked him again and desperately tried to pry his fingers off my neck.

"Let her go," Fennel warned. "I said let her go."

I couldn't turn around to see my partner, which meant he didn't have a shot. And he wouldn't risk taking one. This offender intended to use me as a human shield.

The offender said something in a language I didn't understand and jerked his chin at the door.

"That's not happening, pal," Brad replied.

The bastard squeezed my throat harder, and I clawed at his eyes. *Think, Liv.* Remembering the pepper spray on my keychain, I reached into my pocket at the same moment Brad rushed him. The linebacker held me with one hand and knocked Fennel into the dresser with the other. This guy was unbelievable, but the distraction provided the perfect opportunity.

I grabbed the pepper spray and released it into the offender's face. He dropped to his knees, dragging me to the ground with him. But he lost his hold around my neck, and I shoved him onto his stomach.

"Stay down," Fennel ordered, covering the offender with his gun. "You okay, Liv?"

"Peachy." I coughed and inched away, not wanting to be near the burning aerosol. "You cuff him." Grabbing my gun off the floor, I pointed it at the downed offender, watching as tears streamed down his face.

Fennel took my cuffs and slapped them on the guy. More shots sounded just outside the bedroom door. "How many more are out there?"

The two offenders glared at us. The one attacked Brad spit on my partner's shoe, and for a moment, I thought Brad might knock some manners into him.

"Where are the women?" I asked.

The one I pepper sprayed wiped his face on his shoulder and stared up at me. He spoke again in a foreign language. Even though I didn't understand what he was saying, I got the gist.

"You fucking asshole," I retorted.

He laughed and looked defiantly at me.

"We don't have time for this," Brad insisted.

I tugged open the third door, unsure what I'd find. It opened into an empty bathroom. The window was too small for either man to fit through, and after a quick sweep, I didn't see any obvious weapons or other means of escape. "We can secure them in here."

"It'll have to do." Fennel cuffed the two men together around a pipe to keep them from escaping.

We barricaded the door with a bookcase, just to be certain they couldn't get away or rejoin the fight. It probably wouldn't hold them permanently, but it would do the job until the situation was resolved and more units arrived.

By now, the gunfire had stopped. Afraid of what this might mean, I ran from the room and down the steps with Fennel at my heels. "Upstairs is clear," I announced to the cop slumped near the staircase. He didn't look so good. "Are you hit?"

"I'm fine. He got my vest."

Brad knelt beside him. "How many? Where are they? Where'd they come from?"

"Outside. They got the drop on us. There were four of them." The officer moved to stand and winced. "Tony took down two. The others went down there."

"You're okay. Stay put." Fennel looked around while I requested an ETA. Before dispatch could provide an answer, two additional patrol cars arrived, sirens blaring and lights flashing. Fennel looked up at the incoming officers. "He's been hit. I don't know where his partner is. Sweep this floor, and be prepared for anything. We locked two in the bathroom upstairs."

By the time Fennel finished giving instructions, I was already down the steps. The staircase abruptly ended in front of a steel door. The lock had been broken off, and the door was slightly ajar. Another scream sounded, and I shouldered my way inside.

SEVENTEEN

Bullets flew in my direction, and I dove to the side. The officer to my right used that opportunity to double-tap the offender on the left. The man dropped to his knees, the assault rifle firing a final spread as his muscles tensed before his entire body went limp. He was dead.

The second offender edged toward the back corner of the dark basement. "Stay back," he insisted, pressing the muzzle of his weapon into the ribcage of a scared, red-haired woman.

"Take it easy," I said. "Just put the gun down and let the lady go. We won't hurt you, but you have to let her go."

The officer to my left had taken cover behind a sideways table. He inched to the end and peered around the side. Before I could stop him, he fired. The shot missed, going high.

"Stand down," I ordered, but it was too late.

The offender panicked. He pulled the trigger and darted for a second staircase I hadn't noticed. The two officers lit him up. In slow motion, I watched his blood paint the walls, and then I was moving. I rushed to the woman. She gasped and jerked on the floor.

"Clear."

I heard the declaration, but that was the least of my concern. The officer who took the wayward shot disappeared up the hidden staircase. A few seconds later, he returned. "Clear."

"She needs help. Are the paramedics here?" the officer on my right asked. He knelt beside me, assessing the woman's wound.

"Not yet." I visually swept the room. "The offenders?" I asked the other cop.

"Both down," he said. "Room's clear. What about upstairs?"

"More units are sweeping it now." I held the woman's hand, feeling the tremors coursing through her. "You're safe now. Everything's going to be okay. Can you tell me your name?" But from the look of the wound, I feared my words might be lies.

Her eyes were wide with fright, and she trembled uncontrollably, possibly from pain or fear. "Ma-ma-martha."

"It's okay, Martha. I'm Liv," I said as the other cop checked her pulse. "You're okay. Try breathing with me. Slow. In and out. Just like this." I demonstrated, even though calm was the last thing I felt right now.

"The oth-others." If she kept hyperventilating, she'd pass out. "You have to help them. They aren't safe. He's going to," she gasped several times, "move them."

"Other women?"

She nodded, moaning when the cop pressed down harder against the bullet wound in her abdomen. He met my eyes. The situation dire.

"Where are they?"

She jerked suddenly. "He took them. He took us all. He found us. Made us promises. Lies. So many lies."

"Who is he? What's his name? What does he look like?" I squeezed her hand, hoping to reassure her. "Stay with me, Martha."

Her breath hitched, and she stared at the doorway. I turned to see my partner frozen near the stairs. He had his gun aimed out the door. Until the house was secured, we didn't know who else might be coming, and we weren't going to take any more chances. These assholes got the drop on us once. We weren't going to let them do it again.

I turned the dial on my radio and hit the button. "Are we clear?"

"Not yet. We found a few hidden rooms. Checking for other hostiles now. Hang tight," came the response.

We didn't have time for this. Martha didn't have time for this. "Find the light switch, Fennel. Let's get the overheads on. As soon as the house is secure, we need the paramedics down here."

Fennel ran his hand along the wall, locating a light switch. A single exposed bulb hung from a broken fixture in the ceiling, but it illuminated everything. On the floor in the corner of the room, curled into a ball, was a frail looking girl. She was probably a few years younger than me, and she was dead. A second staircase led out of the room, and the other uniformed officer positioned himself at the foot of it. Blood spattered the walls and floors, and I sneered at the two dead men.

"Martha, hey, how many women did he take?" I asked.

"Six," she swallowed. "Six of us in the room. He'd get us one at a time. Take us to clubs. To meets. But there were always six." She shivered, her eyes glazing over. Even though the room looked like a scene from a horror film, the light helped ease her fears. It kept her talking, or so I hoped. The alternative was she'd lost too much blood and didn't have much time left.

"Tell me about the man. What's his name? What did he look like? Where did he take you?"

"They call him Mr. X. He—" Her head fell back, and her eyes lost focus.

"Martha, stay with me."

She started jerking uncontrollably. "She's seizing," the cop said. "Hold her head."

"Fennel, we can't wait. She can't wait."

My partner turned and raced up the steps. Until the house was cleared, paramedics couldn't enter, but Brad would find a way. Or he'd grab their gear and do it himself. She'd be okay. She had to be.

"Find something we can use," I ordered the other officer. "Towels. Blankets. Anything."

He looked around the room. "I don't see anything." He paused. "I got empty syringes over here and a needle in the dead girl's arm. Do you think she's ODing?"

"Get the Narcan," the other officer instructed while I pulled up Martha's sleeves and checked for puncture marks. "What the hell were these assholes doing to these women?"

Martha stopped seizing, but she lost consciousness. Her breathing came in shallow, ragged gasps, and her pulse was thready. We were losing her.

"I don't know, but we didn't even know he had her. And five more are unaccounted for." My eyes came to rest on the dead woman in the corner. Martha said six, but according to my math, we were up to eight. I didn't want to think how high the number might go.

Heavy footsteps sounded on the stairs, and I drew my weapon. Fennel appeared in the doorway with the telltale blue bag boasting the EMS emblem. He knelt beside us and checked her breathing and pulse. He lifted one of her eyelids and shook his head. I noticed his free hand clench into a fist.

"Is it a through and through?" Fennel asked, and the other cop felt beneath her.

"Yeah."

Fennel blinked. "Okay."

I moved out of the way and let Brad work. We'd all gone through the same first responder training at the academy, but since Brad was former military and had seen combat, he also knew a thing or two about field medicine. Right now, he was her best chance.

I took up watch at the door. A moment later, the other cop returned with the Narcan spray. Since Martha had puncture marks, dilated pupils, and a seizure, we couldn't be certain she wasn't ODing. But I hated to think about the kind of pain she'd be in without the drugs coursing through her system. For a moment, I wished Emma was here. She'd know what to do.

The radio chirped. "The house is clear."

"Send paramedics. We have a woman down. GSW to the abdomen and a possible OD," I radioed back.

The paramedics made quick work transferring Martha to a gurney. In a flash, they went up the stairs and loaded her into the back of the ambulance. I sent a patrol car with them. Given everything that occurred, Martha would be under police protection until we found Mr. X and the rest of the assholes who did this to her.

The officer who'd been shot sat in the back of a second ambulance while the medics tended to his wounds. The bullet didn't penetrate his vest, but he already had the beginnings of an ugly bruise. He'd feel that for the next few days.

I stared at the car. It felt like we'd been under attack inside the house for hours, but it had only been a few minutes. Additional units arrived, and I updated them on the situation and handed out assignments and orders.

By the time I turned around, uniforms were escorting the two men we subdued out of the house. Fennel followed behind them. They weren't talking. Maybe they didn't speak English, or perhaps they were pretending not to understand. Either way, it would make getting answers a lot harder.

"Liv," Brad took a step toward me, just as an echoing crack tore through the chatter, "down." He dove on top of me before the word left his mouth.

Immediately, he rolled to the side, taking cover behind the rear of the police cruiser. Splayed on the ground behind us was one of the two offenders. The bullet impacted between his eyes and covered the officer escorting him down the steps in spatter. Thankfully, he wasn't hit.

"Everyone down," Brad commanded. His eyes scanned the nearby rooftops. "Does anyone have eyes on the shooter?"

I aimed skyward, searching. Another crack sounded. "There." I pointed, just as the sniper grabbed his gun and left his perch. "I got him."

EIGHTEEN

He stared through the scope of the modified hunting rifle. The police would call it an assault weapon, but until now, he'd only used it to put down a few ten-point bucks and several geese. He thought shooting people would feel different, but oddly, it didn't.

He lined up the shot and adjusted to the left. Only one thing mattered; he couldn't kill a cop. That was an automatic death sentence and a line he would not cross.

He fired again. This time, Dmitri went down. He scanned the area. An ambulance had already taken off with one of the women. He wouldn't be able to do anything about that now. The other ambulance remained. Apparently, his people weren't smart enough not to shoot at cops. It's probably why more of his men weren't being hauled outside in cuffs. In fact, he didn't see any of his people, just the two Russians.

The female detective pointed up at him. She and her partner disappeared across the street, taking cover along the buildings. It was time to go. Hopefully, anyone who could lead the police to him was dead.

He grabbed his rifle, slung it over his shoulder, and slid down the exterior ladder. The police were half a block away and closing fast. He didn't have time to waste. They were coming for him.

He reached into his pocket and remotely started his car's engine and unlocked the doors. Jumping inside, he knocked the gearshift into drive and peeled out of the parking space. As he watched the two detectives grow smaller in his rearview mirror, he wished he'd taken care of everything himself. If he'd dealt with Ingrid instead of sending Keith to do it, none of this would have happened.

Instead, his life had turned upside down. He should have gone home hours ago, instead of spending that time outside the motel, fearing the police would return. He knew they'd be back, so he listened to the police scanner app on his phone. If he hadn't been paranoid enough to do that, he wouldn't have known units were rolling on Tremont. He wouldn't have had to shoot Dmitri and Yuri, but he didn't trust them. They'd sell him out on orders from the Russian.

At least the situation was handled. Now he just needed to make final arrangements for the auction. He'd thrown enough parties to know entertainment was key. He'd want distractions, just in case any of the potential buyers turned out to be undercover law enforcement or opportunistic rivals. He'd keep the merchandise caged in the back and take the bidders to see them one at a time. Silent auctions were always best, and this way, he could control the flow of information. Nothing else would go wrong. He wouldn't let it.

*   *   *

"Fuck." Fennel kicked a dumpster as the car sped away. He hit the radio, advising units of the black SUV moving west on Tremont. He called in an airship, but unless it was already in the vicinity, finding the correct black SUV in the city would take a miracle.

I examined the empty spot where the car had been but found nothing out of the ordinary. We checked the sniper's position, but he didn't leave anything behind. A few uniforms joined us and secured the scene. So much needed to be processed, and yet, I didn't believe any of it would lead to fruition.

"You okay?" I asked as we trudged back to the house.

"No. Are you?"

"Not really. I can barely think straight." I stared at the scene before us. Of the six men who opened fire inside the house, only one of them remained breathing, and from the looks of him, that could change at any moment.

"Whoever did this didn't want to leave any witnesses behind. He killed his own guys."

"Are you sure he didn't miss?" I asked. "You pushed me out of the way."

Fennel shook his head. "He wasn't shooting at us. He was shooting at them." Brad squinted into the distance, calculating the trajectory in his mind. He winced. "Are you sure you're okay, Liv?"

I nodded, realizing there was a good chance I'd been in the way. If Brad hadn't intervened, I might be dead on the pavement too. At least we got Martha out, and no cops had been seriously injured. It was a small win, but if I didn't remind myself of it, I'd go mad.

More units arrived, including ESU. The tactical unit swept the neighborhood and started a canvass. Many of the nearby residents came outside to see what the commotion was about. Uniforms taped off the street and kept them at bay.

Fennel headed back inside. Even though CSU had a lot to process, we had to get started. We still hadn't found Clarissa, and time was running out. After everything I just witnessed, I knew it was unlikely we'd find her alive.

"DeMarco," my partner called, "you need to see this."

I followed Brad into the basement. He knelt beside the dead woman and held up a blood-smeared keycard.

I read the name on the card. *Monthly Stay Condos.* "We need to get back there." Slipping on a pair of gloves, I checked her pockets for any other personal effects or an ID, but she didn't have anything else on her. "Do you think he abducted her from there?"

Fennel swallowed. "I don't know. That's the third time this investigation has brought us to that motel. It has to be linked."

"Detectives," a tech called from the hidden staircase, "you'll want to see this."

"I doubt it," I muttered.

Brad looked down at the body. "I'm sorry," he whispered.

He took a deep breath and stood. I recognized his ritual, and I braced myself for what was to come. Fennel led the way up the second staircase. An officer stood off to the side, silently observing everything. The staircase led directly into a room.

"There's no other way in or out," the tech said, "just the stairs."

Dirty sleeping bags and old blankets covered the floor. Several brackets against the wall turned my stomach. Brad nudged the end of a thick rusted chain with the tip of his shoe.

"That's just one of them. We counted four more."

I knelt down, spotting small personal items – a hairbrush, a locket, a compact. "They were kept here. They were prisoners." I felt sick. "But they're not here now."

"No," Brad agreed.

"We'll have cadaver dogs check the property," the tech said.

I nodded. My eyes met Brad's. We'd seen most of the house and heard what Martha said. This didn't read like some sicko kidnapper. This read like human trafficking, making this house a weigh station of sorts. "Did we ID any of the shooters?"

"We're working on it," the tech said. "They didn't have identification on them. The serial numbers on their weapons were filed off, probably bought illegally and obviously unregistered."

"What about the car outside?" I asked.

The tech shrugged.

"Thanks," Fennel said before I could ask more questions the tech couldn't answer. "We want everything bagged and tagged. Every single speck of dust needs to be analyzed."

"Yes, sir."

"C'mon, Liv." Brad nodded at the stairs. "Let's check the rest of the house."

I noted the way his hands shook. The car led us here, but it didn't lead us to Clarissa. I just hoped something inside the house would.

We began upstairs where we apprehended the two offenders. The bedroom didn't contain anything. No clothing. Nothing. CSU would dust for prints and analyze any fibers or trace they happened upon, but I didn't think they'd find much.

The bathroom had a few basic toiletries, and when I opened the cabinet beneath the sink, I found a stockpile of makeup, razors, shaving cream, and hair supplies. "They wanted the women to look pretty." I rubbed my neck. The man who attacked me was in critical condition. His buddy was dead in the driveway. And while I might have wished them harm during the assault, I hoped he'd survive. We needed answers.

Fennel cursed several times. "How long do you think they've been operating in the area?"

"Months, maybe longer." The possibility made me nauseous. My cheek twitched, and I fought to keep the bile from rising in my throat. "I need some air. Can you finish up in here?"

"Yeah." He said something else, but I couldn't hear him over the rush of blood in my ears.

On my way down the steps, I bumped into a couple of crime techs. I quickly gave them a heads-up on what they'd find.

"You should see the main level," one of them said. "It's a mess."

"And don't forget the basement," the other one added. "A real bloodbath took place here. How many firefights were you in, DeMarco?"

"Two, not counting outside. Here and the basement. Ask the other officers what happened on the main level. They'll know." I pushed my way outside, crossed the street, and stared into the horizon. Everything was a mess, and we were just getting started.

NINETEEN

Of the six offenders, five were dead, and one was critical. Their prints came back. They were Russian and Ukrainian. Interpol had a file on each of them, and they were wanted throughout Europe in connection with human trafficking and smuggling.

I stared at their mugshots. I didn't recognize Yuri Paunovic, the one who tried to rip off Brad's head. But the one who attacked me and nearly crushed my windpipe, Dmitri Barkhoff, was our Hardy impersonator. According to Dr. Emerson, he only spoke to Laurel, not Hardy. So I didn't know if the bastard spoke English. Dmitri refused to speak to us in English, but that could have been a ploy. A delay tactic. As soon as the hospital gave us the go-ahead, I'd get answers out of him. One way or the other.

I flipped through the photos, but I didn't spot Laurel anywhere. He remained in the wind. Maybe he was our shooter. Getting caught was never part of the plan. The men who attacked us inside that house might have done so to delay us as long as possible so the sniper and his pals could escape with the women. But when the shooters failed to annihilate the police, the sniper came in and took care of any witnesses. Failure wasn't an option for these bastards, and my thoughts drifted to Keith Richardson. Mr. X must be one sadistic piece of shit. We had to move fast before the body count rose again.

"Mac," I called across the bullpen, "did you get an ID on the tipster?"

She shook her head. "We got the number. It tracks back to an unregistered burner. It was picked up out of state a few months ago. No luck on getting surveillance footage or an ID."

"Dammit."

"You really think one of these chuckleheads called to taunt you? I didn't think they wanted the police involved, especially after what happened."

"I don't know. Maybe one of them grew a conscience, or maybe the tipster is a key witness who knows where the women might be. Regardless, I need to speak to him."

"Did you try calling the number back?" she asked unhelpfully.

"It's disconnected, probably dismantled and ditched. Didn't you ping it for a location?"

Her brow furrowed. "Yeah. You're right. Sorry." She had her hands full with running IDs and checking the neighbors' home security systems for any leads on Mr. X and the missing women.

Changing gears, I went in search of details on the car used in Clarissa's abduction. The vehicle had been dusted for prints. We found three unique sets in the trunk, one of which was a match to Clarissa Berens. Since one set of prints in the trunk matched Clarissa Berens, I knew the other two must belong to other victims. The interior of the car had been wiped. CSU found a few hairs on the driver's seat, which based on length and color probably matched Dmitri. The car wouldn't get us any closer to finding Clarissa or stopping this guy. It was just another waste of time.

Barely any progress had been made on the rest of the house. I rubbed a hand down my face and reached for my coffee cup. I swallowed the remainder, wincing as my muscles constricted. The last time I caught a glimpse of my reflection, I had the beginnings of a bruise. By now, it must be full-blown. That would be fun to explain to Emma and my parents. *Ugh. Focus, Liv*, I chided.

"Did you finish your report?" Fennel asked, returning to his desk.

"Yeah. You?"

"Almost." He clicked something on the computer. "Martha's still in surgery." His eyes were shrouded in darkness.

"Hey," I began, but I didn't know what to say, "you did what you could."

"We have to find them. They shot Martha up with drugs, and when that took too long, they shot her. And they killed the other one with an overdose. They didn't want any loose ends."

"Do we know Martha's last name? Or the other woman's identity?"

Brad shook his head, fighting the emotion off his face. "They don't have records, so fingerprints were a bust. We're running them through the DMV database. Maybe we'll get lucky, but they're probably runaways or strays living on the fringe. No one reported them missing. I checked with missing persons and the FBI. We don't know who they are because no one noticed they were gone." He gulped down some air. "How fucked up is that?"

"This whole case is fucked up." I slammed my hand

against the wall and stormed down the hallway. I couldn't find the missing women. I couldn't stop this on my own. I needed answers. A lead. A miracle. Something useful. And only Dmitri could provide the answers. We needed him alive. He had to make. He just had to.

After stabbing the button on the soda machine a dozen times, I gave it a good kick. The can of sparkling water fell into the dispenser with a loud thud.

"I would wait to drink that," Agent Peters warned. "You should let it settle, or it might explode."

"It's not the only thing." I tapped the top of the can. "What are you doing here?"

"The prints you ran pinged in our system. The FBI's been notified to detain Dmitri Barkhoff."

"Get in line. And good luck getting him to talk. The prognosis isn't good."

Peters rested his hips against the breakroom table and assessed me. "What about the sniper? What can you tell me about him?"

"He killed Yuri Paunovic with a single shot. Nearly did the same to Dmitri, but Officer Gallo intervened."

"Not fast enough."

I glared at Peters. "You weren't there. You don't know what it was like."

"Why don't you tell me what it was like?"

"It's in my report. Maybe if you ask nicely, the brass will let you read it." I tried to push past him, but he blocked the exit. "What do you want from me, Agent Peters?"

"We're working this together, DeMarco. You've uncovered a human trafficking ring, and that's something the Bureau is better equipped to handle. The men who fired upon you are all Eastern Europeans. I've made some calls to our counterparts. They're sending us their files."

"Great."

"I am here to help."

"I know, but that won't bring back the women they've killed or sold."

"So tell me what I can do," Peters insisted.

"I wish I knew. We need to identify the women. Maybe if we figure out when and where they were taken, we'll be one step closer to identifying the man responsible."

"All right."

"And ask Mac about the tipster. Identifying him might put us one step closer to figuring out what's going on."

Peters nodded, and I went out the door. "One last thing, Detective." I stopped and turned. "Good job." Peters said those words without a hint of sarcasm, but the sentiment still felt sarcastic.

"Congratulate me after we find Clarissa and the others and these pigs get what's coming to them."

He brushed his fingers against his neck and jerked his chin at me. "Did someone get a hold of you?"

"Dmitri."

"I'm surprised he made it out of the house alive. That looks serious. Did you have a medic check it out?"

"I'm fine."

"Do your best to stay that way."

Before I could reply, Peters walked away. It was for the best. I was itching for a fight, and despite his attempts to be helpful, the FBI agent had all the makings of a perfect punching bag. Damn. I needed to get out of here before I did something I'd regret.

I spoke briefly to the captain and returned to my desk. "I can't stay here another minute. I need to regroup. Maybe clear my head."

Fennel nodded. "Me too. I'm buying."

"I don't think that's a good idea."

"Yeah, well, I do." Fennel grabbed his jacket and looked around the bullpen. "Cases like this can stretch on for weeks or months. We won't solve it in a night, no matter how badly we want to. If we don't step away, we'll burn out. Actually, it might have already happened. And after everything that went on today, we need to blow off some steam. They'll call if they need us."

"That's why we need to keep a clear head."

"We're not clear now." He made a valid point. "Come on. What else are you going to do?" Again, another good point.

"Fine, but we're not going overboard. This case has taken too much out of us. I can't worry about anyone or anything else. You tell me all the time you don't have a problem, so prove it."

Brad chuckled. "I have a lot of problems, Liv, but grabbing a drink with you isn't one of them."

TWENTY

After a few drinks, Brad and I split a cab. The driver dropped him off, and I changed my destination to the hospital. I wasn't in any condition to work, but I couldn't go home. I needed to fix things with Emma, and I wanted to see how Martha was doing.

I spent hours sitting in the ER waiting room. For once, it wasn't busy, and I took an unobtrusive spot in the back corner beneath the TV. I let my eyes close while I listened to the local station. Given the time, the programming went from infomercials to early morning news. My head bobbed, and I turned on my side and rested my cheek against the wall.

Martha was in the ICU. They wanted to give her time to recover and regain some strength before attempting another surgery. I didn't know what her odds were, and I hated the part of me that wished I'd questioned her harder or gotten more answers out of her before she lost consciousness. She might be the only one who could save the other women, and now, it might be too late.

Dmitri wasn't in any better shape. He coded on the table. They managed to restart his heart, but he wouldn't be talking anytime soon, if at all. The doctors put him into a medically induced coma until they could figure out the best way to deal with his injuries.

At least all the cops made it out alive. CSU recovered four assault rifles, three shotguns, and six handguns. We had been outmanned and outgunned, but we survived. As I drifted in and out of consciousness, I wondered how we could have been so lucky when these women weren't.

"Liv," Emma nudged my shoulder, "what are you doing here?" She looked up and waved at the nurse working the intake desk. "Jen says you've been sitting here for hours. Protection details usually guard patient rooms, not the waiting room. So what's the deal?"

I tried to straighten, but my muscles were stiff and sore. "I'm sorry, Em."

"Have you been drinking?"

"Yeah."

She laughed. "It figures. That's the only reason you ever apologize. Do you want a banana bag?"

"No, I'm not drunk. And I don't think I'm hungover. I just feel like shit, but I am sorry. I just have no intention of doing anything to change it."

Emma plucked a twig out of my ponytail. "Do I want to know?"

"No." But I told her as much as I could anyway. "I don't want to fight with you. And I don't want to worry you or scare you."

"Even after the day you had, you still want to do this?" she asked.

"No. I want to do better. I want to find them. I have to." I turned fully in my seat, and she eyed the bruises in the shape of Dmitri's fingers. "No matter what happens."

"Okay. Wait right here." She went to the desk and spoke to Jen. Then she returned to the chair beside me. "Taxi's coming. It'll take you home. You need to get some sleep. Try some hot compresses. I have a wrap you can microwave in the top drawer of my dresser, and there's a tube of arnica in the bathroom. Do I need to make a house call, or is Brad in better shape than you?"

"He fought a guy, but he's okay." I shrugged. "So am I."

"For once in your life, Liv, do what I say." She gave me a hug. "Now get some sleep."

"There's something else." I bit my lip. Now didn't feel like the time, but I needed to tell her. "I talked to the captain. Until we get this figured out, I'll be staying closer to the action."

"You're going under, again?"

"It's mainly surveillance. We need to keep an eye out."

"Fine, but go home and get some sleep first. Okay?"

"Okay, Em." I let out a sigh, feeling a weight lift off my shoulders. "But only if you promise not to tell my mom about any of this."

Reluctantly, she stuck out her hand. "Deal."

Sleep didn't make me feel any better, but on the plus side, it didn't make me feel worse. After packing a bag, I went to the station. The parking lot was full of federal vehicles. That was never good. I grabbed the two cups from my cup holders and went inside. The conference room was filled with suits and police personnel. This would be about as much fun as a root canal.

Fennel leaned against the edge of the table, and I slipped inside and handed him a cup. "You look about as good as I feel," he said. He looked down at the travel cup. "I brought you coffee too. It's on your desk."

"Not coffee. Emma's hangover cure."

He hid his grin behind the cup. "You made up."

I ignored the comment. "What's going on?" I whispered.

"Interagency task force. Peters didn't want us to have all the fun." He took a sip and jerked his chin at the man giving the briefing.

Since Dmitri had been identified as one of the two men who stole a van from the FBI motor pool and alerts had been issued concerning him and his partner, it wasn't much of a stretch for the Feds to get involved. Furthermore, it was human trafficking, a crime that came with international implications. But since it involved several local homicides, we weren't giving up the case without a fight. We already sunk our teeth into it. If it wasn't for our police work, the Feds wouldn't know about any of this.

"We still haven't IDed the man who jumped off the roof, and we don't know the identity of the woman from the alley. We've handed their information over to the European authorities. Maybe they know something we don't," the agent in charge of the briefing said.

"What about the shooters from yesterday?" Officer Roberts asked. "What do we know about them?"

"We have files on them. The intel is provided in your briefing notes, but suffice it to say, they're believed to work for a human trafficking ring operating in Eastern Europe. At this time, we've only positively identified one of their known associates, an Oleg Vorshkovich. He and Dmitri Barkhoff are the two men who stole the bodies from the morgue. We issued a BOLO for Oleg."

"Do you think he's our sniper?" I asked.

The agent shrugged. "I don't want to speculate."

"What else do you have?" Grayson asked. "And feel free to speculate."

"At this time, we don't have any other names. Our contacts overseas are investigating. Hopefully, they'll help us find a local connection."

"And the women?" I asked.

The agent focused on me, but he didn't answer. "Like I said, we're investigating. The FBI is equipped to handle this."

Captain Grayson turned to look at me. His eyes darted to the door, and I knew the answers wouldn't be forthcoming in this briefing. Luckily, the rest of the briefing didn't take that long. Our support teams would serve the biggest role in the task force. Other than that, it was back to business as usual for the rest of us. Well, most of us.

When we were dismissed, the captain led us into his office and closed the door. "The hospital won't give us access to Martha Evans or Dmitri Barkhoff while they remain critical."

"Are they conscious?" I asked. Maybe Emma could call in some favors on our behalf.

"No." Grayson rubbed his mouth and stared out the slats of the blinds. "The female DB in the basement was another local. Sister Mary Catherine recognized her but didn't have a name. I showed the vic's photo to vice. They recognized her as Claudia Arroyo. She was one of their CIs."

"How is that possible?" I asked. "I didn't think she had a record. Her prints didn't come back."

"She was never formally booked. Detective Lazar worked her the old way." Grayson didn't say much, but since he had been my father's partner, I knew he didn't like it when cops cut corners. "Lazar arrested her, filled out the paperwork, and conveniently lost it when she agreed to work for him. He kept her as a confidential informant, off the books. I pulled her file, but it doesn't provide any identifying information. He swears it's her, and we have no reason to doubt him."

"Who was she informing on?" Fennel asked.

"Local pimps and clubs running girls. Her tips resulted in busts that uncovered other things. Based on the records I've seen, she was making decent money on her tips. When she disappeared six months ago, Lazar figured she made enough and decided to cash out. He thought that's why he hadn't seen her."

"Do you think that's when she was abducted?" I asked. "Have these pricks been operating in our city for half a year without us noticing?"

"I don't know." Grayson stopped speaking when Agent Peters went past his door. "Anyway, I asked Lazar about the Monthly Stay Condos, but vice doesn't know anything about them. They've stayed off the radar, but like I told DeMarco yesterday, since our vic had a room key, we need to check it out. I sent some uniforms to question the employees. No one recognized Claudia Arroyo, and there's no reservation in her name."

"What about cash under the table?" Fennel asked. "When I asked the clerk for information, he made it very clear this is a no-tell motel."

"That's why we're going to conduct some surveillance." Grayson looked at me. "Thanks for volunteering, Liv."

"I have to do something."

Fennel gave me a funny look, noting how the captain grew quiet when a few more FBI agents lingered near his office door. "What's going on, Captain?"

Grayson lowered his voice. "This doesn't feel right. These assholes waltz into the federal building and steal a vehicle, but the Feds know nothing about it. Then when we finally identify one of the pricks, the Feds join our case. It doesn't smell right to me." Grayson thought someone on the inside was involved.

"What do you want us to do?" Fennel asked.

"Stay on it." He looked at me. "Are you sure no one at the motel made you as a cop?"

"I don't think so. I was with Fennel, but I let him ask the questions while I took in the sights."

"All right. Get a room. I'll assign a second team to assist. We're already short-staffed, but this is important."

"What about the connection to the community center?" Fennel asked. "Are we still pursuing that?"

Grayson shuffled through some pages on his desk. "Uniforms were waiting outside when they opened their doors this morning. Claudia Arroyo was never there. We even checked the clinic's records, but she wasn't a patient. Just keep an eye on them, but our focus at the moment is finding the sniper, the missing women, and Oleg Vorshkovich. And I don't believe we'll find them there."

"Even though everything points to strays being taken off the streets by international criminals, Keith Richardson, or whatever the fuck his name is, wasn't Russian or Ukrainian. He was a local. And he targeted these women. We know he worked at the community center and stalked the neighborhood. Maybe these Russian pricks did the same thing. The community center probably wasn't their only hunting ground, but it might be the epicenter," I said.

"Keith probably grabbed the women and delivered them to Dmitri and his pals. But someone, maybe one of the Europeans, forced Keith to kill Jane Doe. And given the dead woman we found inside the house and Martha's condition, I'd say whoever convinced Keith to jump off the roof is part of this human trafficking ring," Fennel added. "We need to find them and question them. These are still our suspects. They tried to kill us. What the hell do the Feds have to do with that?"

"Not a damn thing," Grayson said. "Divert whatever resources you need, but try to keep this under wraps. I don't want Agent Peters or his team interfering with our surveillance until we know what we're dealing with."

"You don't trust them?" I asked.

"I wish I did. But trust has to be earned. We'll see how it goes."

TWENTY-ONE

I tucked my badge into my pocket, combed my fingers through my hair, and touched up my makeup. Mac had put a rush on a new undercover identity. And the department gave me a prepaid credit card registered to my new alias. Hopefully, it was enough to cover the motel's two week minimum stay requirement.

Brad entered the locker room. "What are you doing?"

"Trying not to look like a cop."

"I know that. I meant why didn't you tell me about this cockamamie plan of yours yesterday."

"It's not a plan. It's surveillance."

Brad picked up a tube of mascara. "I didn't realize you had to get gussied up to conduct surveillance." He put the mascara down. "Spill, DeMarco."

"After we spoke to the captain, I made a few calls. It turns out Rogers and Stein has a block of rooms reserved at the motel."

"That makes sense given what we know about modeling agencies and Clarissa's hopes and dreams."

I told Brad about the women I encountered during our first trip to the motel. "I phoned ADA Winters. We got a court order for the motel records. None of the names popped out, but a few of the condos are rented out long-term under corporate accounts. We're running down the businesses now, but if one of them turns out to be a front for these human traffickers, I don't want to risk tipping them."

"So you're trying to blend in with the Rogers and Stein crowd?"

"Or the Clarissa, Martha, Jane Doe crowd," I replied.

"You couldn't attract attention on the street in fishnets and high heels. You really think you'll attract attention with a little mascara?"

"Maybe I'll hang a red light outside my door. That ought to do something."

"What about the room key we found on the body?"

"The strip's been wiped or demagnetized. Whatever Mac said. She couldn't pull any data off of it, so we have no idea what room it unlocked. And the motel staff refuses to cooperate. They claim they don't recognize Claudia." I put on some lip balm. "I hate this."

"I'm coming with you," Brad insisted.

"The hell you are. You spoke to the clerk on two separate occasions. He'll recognize you."

"We'll see about that."

"No, we won't."

Brad reached for another tube of makeup, and I grabbed it out of his hand and swept the supplies into my purse. "In case you've forgotten, I've done my fair share of undercover work. I can disguise myself and blend in just as well as you can, DeMarco." He had a determined look on his face. "Women are disappearing. I won't let that happen to you."

"Maybe it should. That might be the only way we find them."

Fennel sighed and went out the door. After I changed clothes, I found him waiting for me at the stairs. "Grayson's putting a second team on the motel, but Mac's still working on their cover identities. They'll register later tonight, so until then, I'll be staking out the motel from the diner across the street. Should anything occur, I'll be right there."

"You should stay here. We haven't found Clarissa, and time's running out." If it hadn't already.

"You wouldn't be doing this if you thought it was a dead end," Fennel said, "and like I tell you all the time, I go where you go, partner. Plus, it'll give me a chance to question David and a few others from the community center. I hear they have a planning meeting this evening at the diner." He grinned. "Two birds, one stone."

I smiled. "Jerk."

"Be nice and I'll consider springing for snacks."

After selecting a vehicle from the motor pool, Brad gave me a lift to the motel. He dropped me off near the bus stop, and I grabbed my duffel and walked the three blocks to the motel. I looked up at the Monthly Stay sign. This was the place dreams went to die.

The lobby was drab, not nearly as bright or overly commercial like the chain motels. The clerk hung up the phone and asked for my name and information. While I waited for the ancient contraption currently impersonating a computer to verify everything, a large group of blonde women waltzed into the lobby to grab some fresh towels. I'd guess none of them was older than twenty-two, and based on the clothes, shoes, and designer accessories they donned, they had to be models.

"Excuse me," I said, "are you with Rogers and

Stein?"

The nearest woman looked at me. "No."

Before I could ask anything else, the clerk cleared his throat impatiently. "Ms. Torrey," the desk clerk repeated, and I realized I was zoning out, "here is your room key. I have you down for a two week stay, but you can extend it for as long as you need. We offer a continental breakfast from six to ten every morning. The fitness room is on the second floor. Ice machines are on each level. If you have any problems or questions, please let me know."

"Thanks." I took the key. "Room 201, right?"

"Sure thing."

By the time I stepped outside, the women were gone. I glanced across the parking lot in the direction of the diner. Brad sat near the window, watching everything. I went up the steps and slid the key through the slot. When the light turned green, I pushed the door open and turned on the light before entering.

Once I was sure the room was clear, I checked the adjoining door. It led to room 202, but the other side was locked. Based on motel records, no one was staying there. The other surveillance team might want to share the adjoining room, or they'd spread out and find something on the other side of the motel. It was their call, not mine.

Settling onto the bed, I dialed Brad. "Did you see the women?"

"Yes, but I didn't spot anyone I recognized."

"Neither did I, but they fit the profile. I asked, but they denied being part of Rogers and Stein." Getting up, I opened the drape and stared outside. Since I was the first room near the stairs, I had a decent vantage point. Although, I couldn't help but think the first floor might be better, except it was already filled. "Did you see where they went?"

"They went back to their room. They're in 205."

"Okay. Don't let the diner food kill you. I'm going to get some ice and check out the vending machines and see if I can make friends with my new neighbors."

"Good luck."

"You too."

For the middle of the day, the motel wasn't very lively. I grabbed the ice bucket and went to check the ice machine. The drapes were drawn on 205, and the only sounds coming from within were from the television. I considered knocking, but it was too soon. That would be suspicious. I had to be patient. It was the nature of surveillance, and normally, I was better suited to let things play out naturally.

After partially filling the ice bucket, I went up to the top floor and walked the length. The final room, 526, had a sign on the door indicating it was for maintenance. I backtracked to the vending machines and checked their offerings, pretending to have an extreme fascination with various flavors of potato chips before repeating the process on the other levels. On the bright side, the vending machine offerings varied by floor, making my trek less suspicious.

Reading the sign, I slid my keycard into the slot and peered into the fitness room. Two treadmills, a few bikes, an elliptical, a glider, a yoga ball, and a few free weights made up the tiny fitness room. No one was inside, and from the musty odor, I suspected it wasn't particularly popular among the guests.

Eventually, I returned to my room, took a seat at the table, and spent the rest of the day watching for suspicious activity while calling to check on the progress Mac and the rest of the task force was making. My eyes drifted to the diner, and I wondered how Brad was doing.

He remained near the window, but his focus was turned inward. I spotted several new cars in the parking lot and used my phone's camera to zoom in on the plates. I wrote them down on the motel stationery in case we needed additional information.

My mind went back to the anonymous tipster. He knew where the car was, and he wanted us to hurry. He must have known the women would be moved or killed. Or he wanted us to be ambushed. I couldn't decide if he was friend or foe. But the human traffickers had to know we were on to them, which meant they'd be unloading their cargo as soon as possible.

"What the hell are you doing, Liv?" I asked the empty room. At this precise moment, surveillance seemed like the biggest waste of time. And then my phone rang.

"Get over here now," Fennel said.

I pulled the drape, put the do not disturb on the door, and raced across the parking lot. By the time I got to the diner, Brad was waiting in the car. I slid into the seat beside him, and he pulled out of the parking lot. "What's going on?" I asked.

"I don't know. David and those other idiots were talking about fundraising, so I got bored and happened to look out the side window. A group of women got herded into a child molester van. I didn't get a good look at the driver, but he was tall and thin. It might have been Vorshkovich."

"A child molester van?"

"Y'know, the dingy white vans without any windows or logos on them. The kind child molesters use."

"You watch too much TV."

Brad shrugged. "Let's hope that's all it is."

Within two blocks, we caught up to the van. Brad

pulled up beside it, and I recognized the woman seated in the passenger seat. "She's from the motel. Should we call it in?"

"Not yet." Fennel didn't want to tip our hand prematurely. "Let's follow it for a while."

"Okay."

Fennel dropped back, letting a few cars get between us. The driver didn't behave erratically. He obeyed traffic laws to the same degree as most other motorists. He turned, and we followed. The light turned red, and the van stopped. No one tried to escape out the back, but my mind was already on worst case scenarios. My fingers brushed against the radio while my other hand remained poised near my gun.

Brad realized how tense I was. "What did you and Emma fight about?" he asked.

"My job." The light turned green, and I watched the buildings go by. "She's worried about me. And it's your fault. She thinks I should quit my job and do something less dangerous."

"You're joking."

"Nope."

"How the hell could she even suggest something like that?"

"She got the idea from my mom. My mother has been harping on this my entire life. I'm sure my dad's gotten it far worse. She hated that I became a cop. She spent her life worrying about him not coming home, and now she has to worry about me not coming home. When you freaked out Emma, Emma called my mom. The intervention will probably be in a few days. Let me know when you get the invite."

Brad slowed, letting another car pull in between us and the van. "I'm sorry, Liv. I didn't mean for any of this to happen. I just worry about you. About us. I'd hate to see what Emma would do if she found out what went down yesterday."

"I already told her and swore her to secrecy." My eyes narrowed as the van put on its blinker and turned into the valet line for a trendy club.

"How did she take it?"

"We're okay, I think. It probably depends how long-term this assignment is. Do you even think it's worth it? I spent the day in that motel room thinking I should be at the precinct doing something else. I want to be in the vicinity. If I am, maybe this will stop happening and no more women will be taken or killed since I'll be close enough to intervene, but it feels like it's too late for that."

I reached for the radio and asked for details on the van's plate. The plate came back clean. At this point, I didn't know if that was good or bad.

Brad drove past the turn for the valet stand and parked in the first spot he found. Turning around, I watched the women climb out of the vehicle and head into the club. We followed them inside. Half of them crowded around the bar while the other half searched for a table. We scouted the place but didn't spot any persons of interest or any particularly nefarious characters.

"Keep an eye on the driver," Brad said. "I'll speak to the ladies and get the lay of the land."

Forty-five minutes later, I met up with Brad at the front door. "This is a waste of time. Let's call it in. Someone else can sit on this place and make sure the women get home safely. Our priority is keeping an eye on the motel, and with the women at the club, I'll have more time to check out their end of the hallway," I said.

TWENTY-TWO

Room 205 was locked, and when I knocked on the door, no one answered. Unfortunately, the police had no grounds to check inside, and from what Fennel and I observed, the women weren't in any danger. They weren't even here.

Moving down the corridor, I slid the card through the slot, but the light remained red. I double-checked the room number. Maybe I was losing my mind.

I tried the card again. The light on the side turned green, and I pushed the door open. The room was dark, and I flipped on the light and nearly jumped out of my skin. I clutched my chest and slammed the door.

"Well, it took you long enough. I thought you were just going to check their end of the hallway and call it quits," Brad said.

Out of fear and paranoia, I realized I was holding my gun, so I shoved it back into my holster. "What the hell are you doing here? I thought you were camping out at the diner."

"How many times do I have to say it? I go where you go."

"Yeah, right."

Fennel grinned. "David's meeting ended, and after I drank an entire pot of coffee, the waitress was looking to get rid of me."

"What's her name? I should invite her to join the club," I teased.

"Be nice." He stared out the opening in the drapes. "After our excursion to the club tonight, it looks like our play might have changed. Feel like being bait to lure these assholes out?"

"I'm not bait. I'm too old to be bait, as you so eloquently pointed out earlier."

"Regardless, Grayson upped the surveillance since we called for a unit to sit on the club. Obviously, something's going on around here. We just need to figure out what."

"Yeah, I know. So what's the new plan?"

"It's now three teams split between two rooms. You'll come and go, but the other two teams will trade out. If you find a way to get in with the women, do it. That's why we're here to watch your back."

"Great. What room are you in?"

"This one."

"Brad," I warned.

"I'm staying here. No one will ever see me. I'll use the adjoining room to go in and out. Just don't invite anyone back here without giving me the heads-up first, and we'll be fine."

"How did you get inside my motel room? The desk clerk knows you're a cop. You announced the other night."

"You mean last night?"

"That was yesterday? After what happened at the house, it feels like weeks ago."

"Tell me about it."

"Did you badge the desk clerk to get in here?"

"I'm not some newbie boot. I wouldn't jeopardize your cover by doing that. The last thing we need is to tip off the staff. Mac made the reservations online for two last minute businessmen. Loyola and Sullivan showed up to check-in, and Loyola slipped me the keycard for 202."

I opened the adjoining door and peered inside. The other door was open, but the room was dark. "Where is he?"

"Downstairs in 122. The motel had a last minute checkout."

"Did you learn anything at the diner?"

Fennel worked his jaw. "David and his group finished up twenty minutes ago. I tailed him back to the community center. He should be in the middle of hosting another AA meeting. I didn't go in since I wasn't exactly invited back."

"I hate this." I moved closer to the window and peered out the corner where the drape remained open. "Did uniforms question the guests? Did any of them recognize Claudia Arroyo?"

"It's a motel. People come and go. I don't know if they got to everyone."

With a new plan formulating, I dialed the station. We didn't know much about Claudia, but whatever we could find, I'd be able to use. When I checked in, my cover was just a name on a credit card. Now it was time to develop my back story, and I had some ideas. My thoughts drifted to Lyla. No wonder she wanted to be an actress; she could reinvent herself whenever she wanted.

The squawk of the radio drew me from my internal analysis, and I looked up from the computer screen. Fennel remained perched at the window. "Yeah, I got them," he replied. "Any issues?"

"None," came the disembodied voice. "Same headcount you gave us."

"All right. Thanks for the assist." Brad put the radio back on the table and moved to the side of the window, peering out as inconspicuously as possible. "The women are back."

"Now's my chance." I left the laptop on the bed and grabbed the ice bucket. "Go hide in your own room." Fennel saluted as I tucked the keycard in my pocket and went out the door.

I went past 205, stopping at the alcove to fill the bucket with ice. While I listened to the whir of the machine, one of the blonde women ran down the hallway. She took the stairs down, and I peered over the railing. She stopped outside the room where I'd encountered the crying woman on my first visit. She knocked, but no one answered. Slowly, she trudged up the steps, muttering curses.

Taking the full bucket, I stepped directly into her path. "Is everything okay?" I asked.

"No," she mumbled.

"I'm Liv. Is there anything I can do to help?"

She studied me, wondering if she should trust a total stranger. "Shana."

"Nice to meet you." I stood in the middle of the walkway, blocking her path back to her room. "What's wrong?"

After what felt like an eternity, she finally said, "They took her."

The hairs at the back of my neck prickled, and I fought to keep my expression neutral. "Took who?"

"It doesn't matter." She tried to push past me, but I held my ground. "Leave me alone."

"I just want to help. You look upset. What happened?"

"It's not your business."

I squinted. "You have an accent. What is that? German?"

"Czech."

"It's lovely."

She rolled her eyes and scoffed. "Are you hitting on me? I had plenty of men do that in the club. I didn't want any of them, and I don't want you. I'm not here to socialize."

"Why are you here?"

"Work."

"Me too. Modeling, right?"

Her eyes grew wider, confused why a complete stranger insisted on speaking to her. "Yes."

"Thought so. Rogers and Stein?"

Recognition dawned on her. "You were in the lobby asking about them."

"Yeah."

"Is that where you work?"

I chose my words carefully. "I can see why you'd think so."

She analyzed every inch of me. "Talent scout or agent?"

"What's the difference?"

She glared at me and poked at the ice bucket I held in front of my chest. "You took her. You're the reason she's gone. This is your fault."

"Took who?" I repeated.

"A friend of mine. According to Dmitri, another agency recruited her and that's why she left us. That's what keeps happening. Over and over. We all came here together. We were supposed to stay together, get chosen together, but no." Anger burned in her eyes.

"What's your friend's name?"

"Ingrid."

"When did she get recruited?" I asked.

"Last week."

"May I speak to Dmitri?"

"Why? Planning on recruiting someone else?" I saw the jealousy in her eyes. This wasn't concern over her friend's safety; this was animosity for not being chosen. Shana had no idea how fortunate she was.

I had to say something to keep her talking. "Plenty of local modeling agencies have a vast array of openings. I'm not sure how many of you are here, but we have spots to fill. And you'd be perfect."

For the first time since we met, Shana smiled. "Really?"

"Yes."

"You can talk to Ivan since Dmitri's not here. He left on business. He should be back in a few days."

I wasn't going to tell her he wasn't coming back. "Why don't you come back to my room so we can discuss this?"

Before she could answer, the door behind me opened, and a man I recognized as the van driver stepped out of the room. "Shana, get inside."

I turned, smiling brightly. "Hi, I'm Liv."

"I don't give a fuck who you are."

"Ivan, she's with Rogers and Stein," Shana said.

The name meant nothing to him, and I knew this wasn't about modeling. My mind raced, contemplating arguments for exigent circumstances, but I couldn't come up with any. From what little I could see of the room, there were no drugs, no alcohol, and no crimes being committed, even though my instincts said the entire situation was one giant crime in-progress.

"Shana, you don't have to do what he says. We can talk."

"Later. I have to go." She waltzed past me and into the room. He sneered, giving me the once-over, before slamming the door.

I returned to my room and told Fennel everything. With this new information, we needed twenty-four hour mobile surveillance with multiple units. And with Ivan, the new player on the field, we had even more to investigate. We wouldn't be able to keep this from the Feds for long.

TWENTY-THREE

"I don't trust Jaden Miller." Fennel pinned his photo to our board.

"The motel clerk?"

Brad nodded. "There's something about him. He never answered any of our questions. He refuses to cooperate. He doesn't want to be helpful."

"You should be used to that by now, Detective," Captain Grayson said.

"I'm telling you, Cap, he's in on it. He knows what's going on inside. And given the room key we found on Claudia Arroyo's body, the mention of Dmitri, and young women who fit the victimology taking up at least two different suites inside the motel, I don't see what more we need to conduct a raid."

"Ask Winters," I mumbled. The district attorney's office denied my request, and we got into it over the potential ramifications. Needless to say, at the moment, I was their least favorite detective.

"Have you found Ivan yet?" Grayson asked.

"No." I pushed away from the desk. "He's not in

any of the files Agent Peters brought over. The surveillance team snapped a few shots when they went to the club, but Ivan isn't in any of the databases, as far as I can tell. And neither are the women."

"Do you believe Shana's in immediate danger?" Grayson asked.

"I think they all are, but unless Ivan steps out of line or one of the women comes forward, our hands are tied." I stared at the photographs taped to the board. We already had eight victims. Two were dead. One remained critical. And five were still unaccounted for. "We have to stop this. I don't care about making a case. I care about saving them."

"Liv," Brad said softly, but one sharp look stopped him from saying more.

"We have teams at the ready. Nothing will happen to any of the women at the motel," Grayson vowed. "So don't worry about them. Do what you need to do."

After the captain returned to his office, I checked the time. I spent all night waiting and hoping Shana or one of the others would leave the room, but no one did. Around eight this morning, I heard movement in the corridor. Several people went into the lobby to grab the meager breakfast offerings. But Ivan and the women never went down for breakfast. At ten, I gave up and returned to the station.

"Why didn't I ask Shana for Dmitri's last name? If I had, we'd have enough for a warrant. God," I slammed my desk drawer, "why am I so stupid?"

"She probably wouldn't have told you, and even if she did, who's to say he gave the women his real name? From what Martha told us, these men are careful. Mr. X." Fennel gave me a pointed look.

"It could be Ivan."

"We can play this game all day, but it's not helping."

I grabbed a stack of photos off the desk. "I'm going to retrace our steps in case we missed something." I slipped into my jacket and grabbed my keys. "I don't know what else to do."

"I'll go back to the house," Brad volunteered. "I know CSU's analyzed everything, but since our teams found a few hidden rooms, it won't hurt to check again."

"Be careful."

I forced the shiver away, thinking about the sniper and how close we had been to catching him. For a moment, I wondered if Ivan or Oleg had been behind the scope. We barely glimpsed the man before he got into the car and vanished. And with a mask pulled over his face, it had been impossible to determine anything about him.

My first stop was to see Nicky. She was even more panicked now with the constant news coverage concerning Clarissa Berens' abduction. After reassuring her that we were doing our best to find Abigail, I asked about the other missing women. I showed Nicky photos of all eight of our victims, but she didn't recognize any of them.

"Did Abigail ever mention the Monthly Stay Condos?"

Nicky froze; a deer caught in headlights. Finally, she blinked. "What?"

"The Monthly Stay Condos. Does that ring a bell?" Based on her reaction, I knew it did.

"Yeah." She nodded several times. "She used to stay there."

"We didn't see a charge on her credit card."

"I don't know. Maybe she paid cash."

"Did she have that much cash?"

Nicky shrugged. "A lot of babysitting and dog-walking gigs pay cash. Food delivery tends to pay cash too. Abby always had a stack of bills on her. It was easier for her to keep up with how much she had since her income was so unstable."

"Did Abigail ever mention anyone named Dmitri, Oleg, or Ivan?"

"Not that I recall."

I flipped through the photos I brought with me, but I didn't think to grab anything from the FBI files. "Would you mind coming to the precinct to answer a few more questions?"

"This is important, isn't it?"

"It is," I assured her.

"Okay." Nicky checked the time. "I just have to find someone to cover for me. Can you wait a few minutes?"

"That's fine."

Nicky grabbed her phone off the charger and dialed a number. While she did that, I stared out her kitchen window. She lived in a studio apartment that was smaller than the condo at the motel. From things she had said in the past, I knew her biggest regret was not offering to let Abigail room with her. She felt responsible for not helping her friend out. Maybe if Abigail hadn't been so strapped for cash, she wouldn't have crossed paths with Keith Richardson.

After a brief conversation with a coworker, she hung up and turned to me. "Do you think Abby's still alive? The news said the first twenty-four hours are crucial in recoveries."

"Don't believe everything you hear on TV."

She smiled sadly. "You didn't answer the question, Detective DeMarco."

"I don't know, but I promise I won't stop looking for her."

She eyed me for a long time. "Every cop I've spoken to about Abby has said the same thing, but you're the first one I believe. You and your partner." Her brow furrowed. "Franklin?"

"Fennel."

"Right. Sorry." She gestured for me to go first and stopped outside to lock her deadbolt. "Can't be too careful in this neighborhood. Or anywhere. And to think, I used to tell Abby she was too cautious." She followed me to the car and fastened her seatbelt. "It probably should have been me."

"Why do you say that?"

She shrugged. "I used to be wild. Crazy dorm parties. All night ragers. Going to clubs. Hooking up with strangers. Y'know, all the things your parents tell you never to do. When I met Abigail, she never wanted to go out. I used to have to drag her to bars. I always told her to live a little."

I remained silent the rest of the ride, letting Nicky ramble. I hoped she'd say something that would prove useful. She'd been interviewed several times since she filed the initial missing persons report, but she never mentioned the Monthly Stay Condos. So it was possible she had other important information she failed to divulge.

By the time we arrived at the station, I had a lengthy list of questions to ask. I let her settle onto the couch in the breakroom, figuring that would make her feel more comfortable and encourage her to be open and honest. I asked an officer to keep an eye on her while I went to my desk to grab some files.

"DeMarco," Grayson stepped out of his office, "what are you still doing here?"

"I just got back."

"You're done already?"

The question didn't make sense. "What are you talking about, sir?"

"The hospital called. Dmitri's awake. Agent Peters

is on his way. He was supposed to call you."

"Shit." I resisted the urge to race out of the bullpen. "I just brought Nicky in to answer some more questions. She said Abigail Booker stayed at the Monthly Stay Condos." My thoughts splintered. "Hey, Mac, do you have a minute?" I looked back at the captain. "I'll take care of it, sir."

Mac stopped typing and arched an eyebrow at me. "What do you need?"

I gave her a quick rundown of everything that happened. Normally, I'd ask Loyola or Sullivan to fill in, but they were sitting on the motel. And the rest of our unit was busy running down other leads. Plus, Mac was the friendliest face around. I briefed her on what was happening, scribbled down a list of questions, grabbed a hold of the closest uniform, and led them both to the breakroom, After a rushed introduction and apology, I raced to the hospital. I didn't know how long Dmitri would be conscious, but he had answers. And I was determined to get them out of him.

TWENTY-FOUR

"DeMarco," Agent Peters nodded in my direction, "I wasn't sure if you would make it."

"Might have helped if you called."

The FBI agent remained straight-faced. "He's not talking. He's pretending he doesn't speak English. A translator is on the way."

"You think that'll make a difference?" I asked.

"No."

I watched a woman in a lab coat show her identification to the officer outside Dmitri's door before she entered the room, checked his vitals, pushed a button on a monitor, and exited. "How's he doing?" I asked.

"He's stable for now. The swelling in his brain decreased, so we brought him out of the coma."

"What about brain damage?"

"That's a strong possibility. It's too soon to say to what extent," she said.

"Thanks." I watched as she disappeared down the hallway. "Translator or not, it might not make any difference. He could be a vegetable."

Peters stared into the room. "He's faking."

"Where'd you get your medical degree?"

The FBI agent chuckled. "You'll see."

After the translator arrived, we entered Dmitri's room. Despite the bandages and tubes, the bastard still had a spark in his eye. He thought he was playing us.

For the next hour, I went hard at Dmitri, but he wouldn't answer any questions. He wouldn't even acknowledge the translator. I never wanted to beat a confession out of someone before. And now, it took every ounce of self-restraint to keep my hands off of him. I cursed at him, and an amused glint ignited in his eyes. He understood what I said, and he was enjoying this.

"You son of a bitch." I lunged, and Peters pulled me away before I could inflict any real damage.

"DeMarco, take a walk. I want him too, but not like this. I'll take it from here. I'll get him to talk." Peters jerked his chin toward the door.

I stepped out of the room and trudged down the hospital corridor. Losing it wasn't an option, especially in front of an FBI agent. Captain Grayson would have my ass for this, but I couldn't worry about that now.

"Liv?" Emma asked, surprised to see me. "What are you doing here?"

I looked up, not realizing I wandered from the ICU to the ER. "Just questioning a suspect." I leaned against the counter at the nurse's station. "Do you think you can tell me how Martha's doing?"

"Martha?" Em started to type.

"Martha Evans. We brought her in two days ago. Gunshot wound to the abdomen."

Emma clicked a few more keys. "It's still touch and

go."

"Can I see her? Please."

Em looked around and gave me her room number. "You didn't get that from me."

I pretended to zip my lip and wandered back the way I came. Hospital staff typically didn't care about badges. Their priority was treating patients, but since one of their patients was under police protection and the other was under arrest, they allowed me to slip inside without too much fuss.

Taking a seat beside Martha's bed, I glanced at the monitors. Her numbers looked decent. I took her hand and gave it a squeeze. "I'm sorry this happened. I'm sorry we didn't get to you in time."

Closing my eyes, I silently willed her to live. Like Fennel always said, *we promised not to lose anyone else.* Although, no matter how much he wanted that to be true, in this job, it never was.

The officer stationed outside her room stepped into the doorway. "Detective, you should get going. The nurse is making the rounds."

I released Martha's hand, and she let out a wheeze. "Wait."

I clutched her hand again. "I'm here. It's Liv."

Her eyes fluttered, but they didn't stay open. The officer remained frozen in the doorway. "Liv?"

"I'm with the police. I was with you in the house. Remember?"

She squeezed my hand tighter. "The others?"

"Where are they?" I asked.

Her eyes closed.

"Martha, hey, Claudia had a motel keycard. Can you tell me about that? Were you there? What room?"

"107," she whispered, her voice fading as she blinked back out.

"Martha?" I squeezed her hand, but it was no use.

"She said 107," the officer said.

"I'm so glad you heard that." I looked down at her. "Thank you, Martha."

As I was exiting, the nurse came down the hallway. "What do you think you're doing? No one in or out."

"I'm sorry."

"What's your name?" The nurse stared at my badge. "I'll be filing a complaint."

"Yeah, you do that." I reached for my phone. Before I could call in a request for a search warrant, a rush of footfalls came from behind me. I pressed against the wall as half a dozen hospital personnel raced past. When I saw where they were headed, I cursed and ran after them. "What the hell happened?" I asked as Peters was pushed out of the room.

"I don't know. He had this smug look on his face, and then it was lights out." Peters put his hands on his hips and stared through the open doorway while the doctors unsuccessfully attempted to resuscitate Dmitri Barkhoff.

After they called time of death, I stepped away. The tiniest bit of doubt ran through my mind. Did Peters do something to Dmitri? I looked around. "Where's the translator?"

Peters looked dumbfounded. "I don't know."

I took a step back. "This is your mess to clean up. Fix it." Without waiting, I marched out of the hospital. Martha gave us enough to search the motel. We were going to end this today. No one else was going to die.

TWENTY-FIVE

He waited until the hospital alarms sounded before walking away. He should have taken the initiative earlier. He shouldn't have sourced out the work to Keith and the others. But he learned his lesson. From now on, he'd do things himself. He never wanted to get his hands dirty, but he found that he was rather enjoying being in control.

After the detective left the hospital, the coast was clear. He ducked out a side entrance and reached for his phone. "Dmitri's dead. He died from complications. The police are to blame. Make sure your boss knows that."

Oleg didn't respond. Instead, he stared into the cages, trying to decide which woman he'd like to sample. "I'll be leaving after the auction. Ivan's making the arrangements."

"What about the girls at the motel?"

"They are your problem. You found them. You brought them here. You deal with them."

He thought about the stack of VISAs and passports

he had in a safe deposit box. Most of the women in the stable had come from overseas. When they crossed paths with him, he made them his prisoners by taking their papers. They couldn't leave, and they couldn't get other work. They depended entirely on him and the false promises he made. And the local girls who'd willingly signed on the dotted line wouldn't leave because what he offered was far better than what they had before he took them in. The few who did pose problems, like the college student and Clarissa Berens, were caged. He'd unload the troublemakers tonight, and if they didn't sell, he'd eliminate them.

"Who's with the girls at the motel?" he asked.

"No one."

"How many made it to the auction site?"

Oleg glanced into the cages. "Six."

There should have been eight. One remained at the hospital, but she was under police protection. No one was allowed in or out without being on the list. He glanced back at the hospital entrance. It wasn't worth the risk. "The entertainment should arrive soon. I hired an escort service who has agreed to cater in every sense of the word. Make sure security is tight. We don't want any uninvited guests crashing the party."

"Da." Oleg reached into one of the cages and brushed his fingers against the girl's hair. She jerked away, sneering at him.

Hanging up, he called the airlines and made two reservations. The Russian was right; things were too hot. He and his wife needed to go on an extended vacation until things cooled off. They'd leave in the morning with whatever cash he made tonight.

*   *   *

"Keep an eye on him," I insisted, nodding toward the desk clerk, who adamantly opposed the warrant, but a court order trumped any protests he might have. Two uniforms remained in the lobby while Miller phoned his boss. "Fennel doesn't trust him."

I watched officers corral the six women from room 107 into a secluded portion of the parking lot. Until we concluded the search, they weren't going anywhere. As of yet, not a single one provided an ID. I looked around, but I didn't spot any sinister looking men. Wouldn't the women have been kept under lock and key if they were part of a human trafficking ring?

Huddled next to a cruiser stood the crying woman I encountered on my first trip to the motel. At least she hadn't been taken and had stopped crying, but now, she looked terrified. She was white as a sheet, her eyes darting to and fro as she trembled slightly. Two of her friends flanked her, running their hands up and down her arms in an attempt to comfort and warm her.

I moved closer to the group. Luckily, no one recognized me beneath the tactical gear and face mask. I didn't want to risk being spotted since we only had access to the one room. "Is she okay?" I asked the officer guarding the group. He shrugged, and I let out a huff. "Just keep an eye out. Something has her spooked."

Several guests stepped out of their rooms to see what was happening. I spotted Shana and a few of the other alleged models. "Hey," I whispered to the closest officer, "go upstairs and ask for IDs. I have it on good authority they might be here without the proper documentation."

"You realize this is a sanctuary city, right?"

"I'm not telling you to call ICE or even that they're illegal. I'm just asking you to get some facts straight. If a crime is being committed, it's your duty to stop it."

This was a fine line. "And watch out for a guy named Ivan. We need to bring him in. Find a reason."

The officer nodded and went up the steps to join the others who were doing their best to herd the onlookers back into their rooms while we conducted the raid. Fennel pulled to a stop and got out of the car. I waved him over, and he did a double-take.

"Liv?"

"Yep."

"Nice look."

As soon as we got the all clear, Brad and I entered suite 107. The two double beds were unmade, and the pullout remained open. A few suitcases and backpacks lined the corners of the room. Although, technically, the room could hold six, it was a tight fit.

"I'll start over here." I entered the bathroom, regretting my decision.

The counter wasn't even visible beneath all the products. Rolling the mask up so I could see better and breathe, I started in one corner. We needed proof Martha or Claudia had been in this room. The officers outside were taking statements, asking the women questions, and showing them photographs. We were close. We just needed a little cooperation, but from what I'd seen, the women were more afraid of us than whoever was responsible for the disappearances and murders.

After finishing in the bathroom, I stepped into the bedroom area and opened the closet door. "More bags."

"And to think, they packed light," Brad teased from the other room.

I crouched down and unzipped the first bag. It contained nothing but the essentials. I checked for luggage tags and IDs but came up empty. I tossed it to the side and pulled out the next bag. And then the next. I just finished checking the third bag when I spotted a rolling suitcase. I pulled it out, finding it locked. The search warrant covered everything in the room. The lock didn't mean a thing.

I made fast work with the bolt cutters and unzipped the suitcase. I reached for the first leather case and lifted it out of the bag. Flipping it open, I stared down at a perfect replica of an FBI badge and photo credentials.

"I got something," I called.

Fennel entered the room a second later, and I held up the fake badge. He took it in his gloved hand and flipped to the photo. "Laurel, or should I say Oleg Vorshkovich?"

"And here's Hardy, aka Dmitri Barkhoff." I held up a second ID. Digging deeper in the bag, I found an array of uniforms, more fake credentials, and additional props. "What do you make of this?" I held up a pair of scrubs and a lab coat. "Check the tag in the neck."

Brad put the fake FBI badges down and examined the articles of clothing. "Property of Breckenridge Community Theater." His eyes narrowed. "That's the same theater house where Lyla performed."

"This isn't a coincidence." I rifled through the bag, finding more props and costumes.

With a solid lead and an obvious connection, the officers placed the six women under arrest. They were loaded into the backs of three cruisers and taken to the station. At least they'd be safe there.

Fennel and I continued to search the room for additional evidence and items of interest. "Berlin?"

"That was the snow globe we found next to Jane Doe."

He held up a cloth bag. Stitched to the front was a patch that read *Berlin*. He emptied the bag and pulled out a wallet. "No ID." But there was a photo inside. He took it out, and sadness and anger flashed across his face.

"What is it?"

"Family photo, maybe?"

I took the picture from him and looked at it. Jane Doe and a woman who looked like an older, heavier version smiled brightly at the camera. Jane Doe wore a pink leotard and matching wrap sweater, and the woman I assumed to be her mother held a bouquet of roses.

"She was a dancer." I flipped the photo over but there was nothing written on the back. From the creases and frayed edges, I knew the photo had been carried a long time. "Maybe Mac can pull something useful from the background."

"Yeah, maybe." Fennel didn't sound convinced. "But that proves it. Jane Doe was here. The bastards who took her and probably killed her were here." He peered out the window, but the women had already been taken away. "One of them knows what happened."

"They weren't the only ones here. Martha and Claudia must have stayed here at some point."

Brad finished examining the last suitcase and ripped off his gloves. Stuffing them into his pocket, he stormed out of the room and straight to the motel office. An officer stepped inside the suite to assist, and I told him we were finished and CSU would need to process everything. Then I slid the mask over my face and went outside, hoping my partner wasn't doing something stupid enough to get himself suspended.

"Detective," an officer stopped me before I could follow Brad, "you were right. The women upstairs in 205 don't have any IDs. Some have accents. I asked about their passports, but they couldn't supply them.

However, since they have open bottles of liquor and they can't prove they aren't minors, we can take them in until we determine their ages. It's not much, but..."

"What about Ivan?"

He shook his head. "No men around."

"Fine. Take them in. After we determine who they are, we'll be back to serve a second warrant." Out of the corner of my eye, I saw Fennel slam his palm against the counter. "I have to go." I dashed across the parking lot and into the office.

"How do I know you aren't responsible?" Fennel asked. "The names you have on file are bogus, and you refuse to cooperate. We've already found two women dead. A third's in the hospital. That's three strikes right there. And that doesn't even take into account the kidnapping charges. And I'm just getting started. I'll give you a second to think about your answer. Maybe you happened to remember something." Brad waited.

I remained near the door, doing my best to look menacing, which was a much easier feat while dressed head to toe in tactical gear. The desk clerk looked at me then at the glass door on the other side of the office. He was going to run.

"Do it, and I'll add fleeing the scene and resisting arrest to the growing list." Brad gave him a daring grin.

"Fine." The clerk spun the ancient CRT monitor around and placed the mouse on the upper portion of the counter. "Those are our records. Look all you want. Like I said, I don't know who rented the room. It says full occupancy. Those are the charges. That's all I know."

"I doubt that." Fennel printed the entire guest registry anyway. We had everything — names, corporations, vehicles, number of guests, and charges.

I took the stack of pages and skimmed them, but it was the same information we received when serving the initial court order. "What about your off the books visitors?"

Miller reached beneath the counter and pulled out a thick yellow book. He slapped Brad across the face with it and bolted for the side door. Brad caught him and threw him on the ground before he even made it out of the lobby. I picked up the phonebook from the floor.

"You realize cops have a reputation for beating uncooperative suspects with phonebooks. Are you trying to give us tips on how to do our job?" I quipped.

The clerk glared as Brad cuffed him. "Bite me, bitch."

Brad and I exchanged a look. Before we even got our suspect out of the office, a few of the maids came to see what was happening. I questioned them while Brad passed the clerk off to another officer. At this rate, we might run out of police cars.

TWENTY-SIX

After everything we found and the clerk's outburst, we shut down the motel. The guests were asked to vacate temporarily, and additional court orders were already in the works. The precinct was abuzz with activity. Our holding cells were at max capacity, and every interrogation room was occupied. Officers were stationed outside every room. The women thought we were out to get them. They didn't realize we were protecting them.

"They don't know what's going on," I said. "Shana thinks they're being selected for jobs, and the others disappeared because they got their big break."

"C'mon," Fennel nudged me toward the car, "we have to move. As soon as the men responsible return to the motel, they'll realize they've been made. We have to act fast. We need actionable intel, and right now, our best lead is the community theater."

"Community theater. Community center." I let out a displeased growl. "These are supposed to be safe places, not fronts for human traffickers." I palmed my keys and climbed into my car. Brad tapped the side before getting into his own cruiser.

A few minutes later, I parked in the loading zone behind the building. Two vans had their hazards on, and I spotted David Hennen unloading something from one of the vans. I stepped out of my car just as Brad parked at a diagonal, preventing the two vans from leaving.

"Mr. Hennen," I called, holding up my badge, "I need a moment of your time."

He put the heavy box down and dusted off his hands. "What can I do for you, officer?"

"Detective DeMarco," I corrected.

"Mind lending me a hand, Detective?" he asked, lifting the box.

"I do."

Hennen ignored me and continued into the building. Fennel checked the vehicle, and I cautiously followed Hennen inside, insisting that he stop, put down the box, and turn around slowly. After an inevitable protest, he sighed and obeyed my commands.

"What are you doing here?" I asked.

"Making a delivery. Some kids in the afterschool program help with set design." He opened the box, revealing art supplies.

"Do you make this run often?"

"Whenever we receive donations." Hennen looked behind me as my partner entered the building. "This is harassment, bordering on stalking. The two of you are violating my civil rights. I want to speak to your supervisor."

"David Hennen, you're under arrest," Fennel said, surprising me with that statement. "You'll be able to speak to our captain after you're booked. Turn around, and put your hands behind your back."

"On what grounds?" Hennen challenged.

Brad held a glove in his hand, the latex edges wrapping around a student ID. Lyla James' student ID. "This was in the back of your van."

Hennen stared at it, but he didn't move. Fennel closed the distance between them in moments, spun Hennen around, and cuffed him. He led him out of the building, reading him his rights on the way to the car. Once Hennen was secure in the back, Brad turned to me.

I stared at the open doors on the van.

"It was in plain sight. Right there." Fennel pointed. "I already radioed it in. We'll impound the vehicle." He glanced at the second vacant van. "I didn't see anything damning inside that one, but CSU might. Where's the driver?"

I spotted Jesse, the man I met in AA, taking a smoke break at the side of the building. "I got him." I headed toward the side of the theater. "Take Hennen in and get us some damn answers."

But as usual, my partner wouldn't leave me without backup. He remained outside the car, prepared to intercede should the situation require it. Hopefully, Jesse wouldn't pose a problem.

"Jesse," I called, approaching slowly from the side. My hand automatically rested on the handle of my gun.

"Hey, I know you." He smiled. "Liza? Lidia?"

"Liv." I held up my badge. "Detective Liv DeMarco."

"No wonder you gave me the third degree." He chuckled. "Be honest. Do you even have a drinking problem?"

"No, but I have a very big problem. And I hope you can help me with it."

He snubbed the cigarette out against the brick wall.

"Sure. How can I help?"

"Is that your van?" I pointed. "Did you drive it here?"

"I drove it, but it's not mine. It belongs to the community center. David asked me to help out."

"To do what exactly?"

Jesse told me the same thing Hennen did regarding their trip to the community theater. While he was speaking, a patrol pulled up. I waved Brad off. Jesse watched the exchange uncertainly.

"What's going on?"

I didn't trust him. He could be an accomplice. "Would you mind showing me the van and the supplies you're delivering?"

"Sure, no problem."

I waited for him to go first, keeping a close eye on him in case he presented as a threat or decided to bolt. A cursory examination of the second vehicle didn't turn up any evidence that Lyla or any of the other missing women had been inside. Jesse opened the boxes, and I used the tip of a pen to pick through the contents, finding nothing but paints and brushes.

Two tow trucks arrived, and the vans were sealed and loaded onto the beds. "Where are the boxes you already unloaded?" I asked.

"Inside. Let me show you." Jesse headed for the door, and I followed him. An officer remained near the theater's rear exit. "In here." Jesse flipped a light and pointed to a backstage storage room. "We put them right there."

They contained more of the same. "Jesse, I need you to come to the station and answer some questions. As long as you cooperate, you won't be in any trouble." That last part might have been a lie, depending on the things he said, but it wouldn't help to run through worst case scenarios now. The last thing I needed was a possible witness or lead to lawyer up.

He looked down at his watch. "When?"

"Now."

"I actually have to go to work now."

"I'm sorry. This can't wait. We'll get you in and out as quickly as possible, I promise."

He thought for a moment. "What is this about?"

Before I could answer, I heard a squeal come from the corridor. I poked my head out of the room and saw a gray-haired woman roll a rack of dresses down the hall. One of the wheels let out another shriek, and I cringed. "Excuse me," I called. She jumped, startled. "I'm with the police. Who are you? And what are you doing?"

She looked at me as if the questions didn't compute. "I'm Gwen. I work here."

"What are those?" I asked, pointing to the rack.

"Costume donations." She stepped closer, spotting Jesse lingering in the doorway behind me. "Hi, Jesse. Bring us anything good today?"

"Just more painting supplies for the kids' theater group."

Hearing our voices, the officer entered the building to see if everything was okay. "Detective?"

"Did they finish outside?" I asked, and the officer nodded. "Do me a favor and take Jesse down to the station. Tell Grayson he might have important information. Fennel has the details. We want to get him in and out as quickly as possible."

"Ma'am?"

"Go," I insisted. I turned to Jesse. "I don't want to hold you up longer than necessary. Go with the officer. When you're finished, someone will give you a ride to work or wherever you want to go."

He held up his palms. "Yeah, okay. Whatever."

The woman watched the exchange, her jaw hanging open. When the two men were gone, she found her words. "Can I see your badge?"

"Sure." I unclipped it and held it out to her.

She examined it closely. "It's heavier than I thought. The props we use around here are a lot lighter. They're nothing but tin. This has a nice heft."

"What can you tell me about Lyla James?" I asked.

Understanding registered on her face. "Oh. You still haven't found her? When no one else came by to ask questions, I just thought, y'know, maybe she'd been found."

"Not yet, ma'am. I'm following up on some leads. What can you tell me about these donations you received? Did you ever notice anything suspicious about them or the people who brought them?"

"No."

"What about David Hennen?"

"David's a gem. He does a good job getting the word out and collecting materials. He always sends someone over from the community center to bring us the deliveries, even though we have our own pick-up guys."

I'd seen the theater's records before. Missing persons had collected them and checked all the employees and volunteers when they were investigating Lyla's disappearance. But Lyla's ID ended up in the back of that van somehow.

"Did Lyla ever make a delivery? Jesse said she hung up posters inside the community center."

"She might have. She loves theater. A real thespian." The woman smiled. "I already showed the other cops the dressing rooms and prep areas, but you're welcome to look around if you think it might help."

I doubted it, and I didn't want to waste too much

time. "That's okay, unless Lyla had a locker or cubbyhole where she kept things."

"We don't have any designated spaces, but I'll show you the spot in the changing area Lyla used."

Unfortunately, nothing she said explained how Lyla's ID ended up in the back of the van. I was fairly certain it was because Lyla had been in the back of that van, probably when she was abducted, but unless CSU found blood in the back, the evidence remained flimsy.

A shiny dress hung from the peg on the wall where Lyla hid behind a paper screen to change. "Did she wear this?"

"Yes, for the dance number at the end."

"Kind of high-end for community theater, isn't it?" I examined the designer label, but it wasn't a knockoff.

"More donations. I believe that piece came from Rogers and Stein. They were having a charity auction, and David convinced them to donate a lot of their old pieces and office materials that didn't sell. A lot of our costumes and equipment we use on stage, lighting, cameras, even the curtains, came from Rogers and Stein. They just renovated and got rid of everything." She opened the closet door, pointing to feather boas, dozens of masks, and various other props. "Can you believe they had all this just lying around from past photoshoots? Their renovation has been great for us."

"What about these?" I showed her photographs of the costumes and badges I found in the motel room. "Where did they come from?"

"I can't be sure. We do take other donations, and we also have a budget we use to purchase whatever we need. It isn't much, which is why donations are so appreciated." She narrowed her eyes at the badges. "As far as I know, we've never used props like that in any of our productions. We normally use these." She showed me an array of shiny tin stars. "They might not be authentic, but they're visible to the audience. Those would be too small."

"Yeah." I glanced back at the shiny dress. "Rogers and Stein," I repeated. "By any chance, do you remember who exactly made the donation?"

She shook her head. "I would guess someone in PR."

"That's what I was thinking."

TWENTY-SEVEN

"You, again?" The bitchy receptionist from last time rolled his eyes. "What do you want now?"

"I need to speak to whoever's in charge of donations."

"Donations?" He tapped a few keys, muttering under his breath, "You look like a charity case." With a fake smile, he added, "Mr. Stein authorizes all our charitable contributions, but he's in the London office this week. You'll have to come back."

"Okay, then I'll need to speak to whoever's in charge of these renovations."

"Honey, it's five o'clock. Everyone who's anyone has already left for the night."

"So that's why you're still here?"

"Me-ow," he replied.

I leaned closer. "Look, you're a smart guy. Surely, you have your finger on the pulse of this place. You must know everything that goes on around here."

He raised an intrigued eyebrow. "Maybe."

"Young women have been disappearing lately. One

of them was found dead right outside this building."

"Seriously?" His ears perked up.

"Yes." I removed my phone from my pocket and scrolled to the proper photos. "Do you recognize any of these people?"

He flipped through the images, shaking his head. "They don't work here."

"What about as temps?"

"I don't exactly mingle with the temps."

Of course not, I thought miserably, *that would be beneath you.* "Models? Or model wannabes?"

He snorted. "We get plenty of those. They're a dime a dozen. I definitely wouldn't remember any of them."

This was getting me nowhere. "Is Mr. Crenshaw here?"

"No, he's been out sick the last two days."

"Do you know anything about the donations made to the community theater?"

"Sorry." He pointed to the clock over my head. "Time's up. If you'd like to make an appointment to speak with someone, call back in the morning."

Frustrated, I handed him my card. "If you remember anything, give me a call. I'll make it worth your while."

"I doubt you could. And this game is tired and boring, kind of like you."

Before leaving the building, I spoke to the woman in the lobby. She'd been helpful enough to photocopy the office directory for Brad, and today, she handed me the sign-in sheet. At least I had a list of deliveries and pick-ups. But tracking down each service and driver and asking questions would take forever. However, as my dad always said, police work required patience and perseverance. *Stick with it, Olive. You got this.*

I returned to the car and flipped through the pages,

dialing numbers and asking questions as I went. By the time I looked up, it was dark out. My phone beeped, and I checked my messages. Mac left a text. Nicky hadn't been able to provide any useful information. Fennel hadn't called, which meant Hennen hadn't said a word. I sent my partner a message and asked about Jesse, but that turned out to be another dead end.

Now that we had the women from the motel, the human traffickers would scatter. And whatever cargo they still possessed, they'd have to liquidate immediately. Units had the motel under surveillance, but no one had returned to the scene of the crime. They had probably been tipped by the circus of police vehicles present earlier in the day. Mr. X and his minions must have rabbited.

I needed to get back to the station. The answers were there. Shana or one of the others had to know something. They'd be able to tell us where they came from, who the men were, and what they were promised. I sighed and turned the key in the ignition.

As I headed away from the office building, I drove through the same neighborhood Brad and I had initially staked out. The crime scene tape had long been removed from where Keith Richardson had plummeted to his death. I turned down the next block, heading away from the apartment buildings and toward the nearby bars and clubs.

I had just passed the restaurant where Lyla worked when I spotted a group of women entering a nearby warehouse. Clarissa? I blinked. Surely, I must be seeing things. At this point, all young blondes looked like victims to me, but it was worth checking out.

I slowed, circling the warehouse. The nearby spaces were occupied with high-end vehicles and chauffeured cars. Several warehouses had been converted into clubs or pop-ups for raves or other party venues. But this wasn't the trendy part of town. I radioed, advising dispatch I was checking it out, and found a nearby space.

Three men in suits went to the front entrance, but the women I'd seen had gone through the back. The front door had a surveillance camera and a keypad. The men looked up. One of them held something up to the camera, and the keypad illuminated. After entering a code, the door opened. Obviously, this was invitation-only, and I'd left my invite at home.

For the next twenty minutes, no one went in or out. The waiting made me twitchy. I didn't see anything suspicious enough to bust in, guns blazing. I needed something concrete besides a passing glimpse of a young blonde woman. Even though my gut insisted Clarissa Berens was inside, I'd have a hell of a time proving it if I were wrong. Still, I knew I had to get inside.

Tucking my badge and gun into my purse, I hefted the bag over my shoulder and headed for the back door. Unlike the front, it didn't have security or guards. I pushed the door open as quietly as possible.

It was darker inside than outside, so I didn't notice the man who snuck up behind me until it was too late. He pushed me toward an inner doorway.

"What are you doing in here?" His slightly accented voice made the hairs at the back of my neck stand at attention. "You need to change."

"Change?"

He shoved me into another room and locked the door behind me. It took a moment for my eyes to adjust. I was in a dressing room. A vanity sat in the corner with makeup and hair supplies. A rack of mini-dresses stood in the middle of the room. What the hell was this place?

I banged against the door. "You're making a mistake. Let me out."

But the man on the other side didn't respond. I tried twisting the knob, but it was locked. I could break the door down and go back the way I came, or I could see what was behind door number two. I chose door number two.

Peering into the hallway, I watched the strobing neon lights through a haze of cigarette smoke. So this was a club. I took a step out of the dressing room, and a woman in her too low, too short cocktail dress nearly collided with me. I didn't recognize her, but she seemed anxious.

"Hurry, they want us out here to serve and entertain. You can't do it dressed like that."

"Who are you? What's going on?" I asked.

She pursed her lips. "Go get changed."

Again with the changing. "I'm a cop. What is this place?" I asked.

She laughed. "Right, you're a cop. Keep dreaming, sweetie."

I showed her my badge while keeping an eye on the action. The businessmen I'd seen enter earlier were now at a table, talking amongst themselves and drinking. A few more were at the bar. Some were flirting or making out with a few of the women. A few others were dancing. The one glaringly obvious discrepancy was the men outnumbered the women four to one. In the clubs I'd visited, that was never the case. But the women weren't here to party; they were working.

"Answer the question."

"Oh, yeah. That looks so real," she scoffed, "like they'd really let a cop in here. You found it in the back with the other costumes and outfits, didn't you? Personally, I would have gone with the naughty nurse uniform."

For a moment, I felt like I was in the *Twilight Zone*. Before I could protest, a man came up to us from behind one of the thick velvet curtains that served to soundproof and hide the ugly graffiti and cement walls. With one look at him, I knew I was in the *Twilight Zone*.

"There you are," Axel Kincaid practically purred. He looped his arms around my waist, grabbed my badge, and shoved it inside my purse, zipping the bag before anyone noticed my gun. "Play along," he whispered, an urgency to his tone. I reached for my bag, and he grabbed my hand. "That's enough. I just wanted to make sure you could role-play." He smiled at the woman and nuzzled my neck. "She's good at it, isn't she?"

"Very good. Now get changed." She gave me a hard look and vanished into the crowd.

Axel pushed me back into the changing room and closed the door. "How did you get in? I've spent the better part of an hour looking for a way out. Where's your partner? Is your backup outside?"

"I don't have any."

"Fuck." He rubbed his eyes. "Why not?"

I shook off my confusion. "What is this place? Some new underground club you're scoping out?" Since Kincaid ran an exclusive, members-only club, I couldn't help but think he was here to check out the competition. He might have wanted the police to shut it down for purely selfish reasons.

He loosened his tie and unbuttoned the top button, as if the confinement was adding to his stress. "I don't know what this place is, but it isn't good. We have to get out of here."

"What the hell are you even doing here?"

"Don't." His ice blue eyes blazed. "You came to me

for help, remember?"

"I asked if you knew anything about a car."

"And someone tipped you about that, right?" He moved closer, and my hand automatically went for my gun.

Even though my investigation into Axel Kincaid resulted in him being officially cleared of any suspicion, he was a car thief by trade with a violent past. I didn't trust him. He was a club owner, who boasted creating the 'Vegas experience' by getting anyone just about anything. I had no doubts he ran drugs and possibly girls out of Spark, but I needed answers and thought he could help. I just didn't expect to find him in the midst of my investigation.

He grabbed my wrist. "I'm not the enemy, Liv. You don't need to be afraid of me."

"That tip nearly got me killed. Who called it in?"

He searched my eyes for a moment. "You're serious?"

"Yes."

"It doesn't matter who called. He didn't try to harm you. And for the record, that wasn't my intention. You asked a question, I answered. It's that simple."

"What is this place? How'd you find it?"

"I'm not sure what it is, but it's dangerous, especially for women."

I jerked my hand out of his grip and took a step back. "Why are you here?"

"I hear things. According to the whispers, this is the ultimate experience. It's only available to serious, hardcore thrill-seekers." He took a step back, sensing I wasn't comfortable with his proximity. He watched the suspicion dance across my face. "Check your phone."

Keeping one eye on him, I fished out the device. "No signal."

"They're using jammers. All cell phone and radio signals are blocked. Did you notice the heavy hitters? The exits are covered by former special forces guys with automatic weapons. No one's going anywhere. We need another way out."

"How many guys?" I moved toward the door. I had to get the lay of the land. Was this a hostage situation?

"I counted four." He stopped me before I could open the door. "You go out there like that, and they'll kill you on sight. You need to get out of here."

"I need to get these people out of here." I cracked the door open and peered out. I could make out the outline of two guys near the front. "Where are the other two?"

"They're at the side door. It's to your left."

I pressed my cheek against the doorjamb, but at this angle, I couldn't see that far. But no one acted worried. It appeared everyone was having a good time. I spun, assessing Axel. Spending three months imbedded in his club meant I'd gotten to know him. I could tell when he was stressed, and right now, that dial was cranked to eleven. I just didn't know if it was because I interrupted the party or if he actually feared for his life.

"Tell me everything you know." I shut the door and moved to the rear of the room. The door I'd been forced through earlier remained locked, but since it might be our only way out, I'd find a way to open it. "Who's in that room? Who are the women?"

"From what I gather, they're part of a service. A cross between escorts and catering."

"You ever hire them?"

His tone turned cold. "No, Detective."

"And the guests? The men drinking and dancing, what about them?"

"I know a few."

I twisted the knob, but it didn't budge. I knelt down and removed the lock pick kit from my purse. "Do they have names?"

"Yes." He eyed the lock. "You're not going to get that open. It's state-of-the-art. Bump proof, pick resistant. I have the same model on my doors."

A noise sounded from deeper inside the warehouse, and we both froze. I pulled my gun and aimed at the door, but whoever was outside reconsidered. I turned my attention back to the lock.

The first thing I had to do when we got outside was call for assistance. ESU would have this place surrounded in minutes. I tucked my gun behind my back and moved to the rack of dresses. A metal bar ran across the top. It was held in place by thin, flat metal brackets.

"I need names. Did someone invite you here? How'd you know how to get in?" I tossed the dresses to the side while I struggled to figure out how to disassemble the rack.

Axel moved closer to assist, and together, we manipulated the main bar out of the side joint. "I'm not a rat, Liv."

"I don't care what you are. I want to know why you're here and how you got inside."

He didn't answer. Instead, he met me at the locked door and took the flat metal square from my hand the moment I pulled the pin free from the bottom hinge. He worked the flat metal between the pin and the hinge at the top, a much easier feat for him since he was significantly taller.

"Axel, talk to me."

"The invite went out yesterday to a certain clientele. It listed the time and location." He pulled a sheet of paper out of his pocket and held it out. "That got me inside."

I looked at the paper, but it didn't provide any details, just the cryptic message and the promise of a once in a lifetime opportunity. "Is Clarissa Berens here?"

"I don't know."

I saw the guilt in his eyes. "Tell me what you do know."

"So you can arrest me?"

"I might do that anyway."

He let out an unhappy harrumph.

"What did you hear or see, hypothetically?" I asked.

He finally pulled the pin free. Now we just had to remove the door from the wall. The lock would remain locked, but it wouldn't matter with the door no longer attached. "It's possible a former member of Spark said women were going up for auction tonight. I convinced him to give me the address and the entry code." He nodded at the paper. "Let me be clear. This is his invitation. Not mine. And for the record, I'd like to get the hell out of here."

"Who told you about this? Why didn't you report this to the police?"

"It doesn't matter."

"It fucking does." We pulled the door free, and I slipped into the narrow hallway. It remained dark, but the bastard who locked me inside wouldn't get the jump on me again. "Stay behind me."

"Liv," Axel protested, "we have to get out of here. These men mean business."

"Do you know who they are? Do you know Mr. X?"

"Mr. X?"

For the briefest moment, I feared Axel could be Mr. X. Maybe he was going to all this trouble just to get me out of the way, so I couldn't interfere in any more of his illicit dealings. I glanced behind me, seeing the reflective gleam of the metal bar he carried like a bat.

Any minute, he could bash my skull in.

"Yeah, one of the women identified him." I waited for Axel to swing, but he didn't. Instead, we made it to the exit without incident. Obviously, the man who locked me inside must have left. "We just need a name."

"I can't help you."

"Can't or won't?"

But he didn't answer.

Once outside, I reached for my phone, but we were still too close to the jammers. I couldn't get a signal. I took a step toward the car, but I heard gunshots. Normal people ran from gunfire. Cops were trained to run toward it.

"Call for help," I ordered before turning and racing back inside.

TWENTY-EIGHT

The sound had been muffled, but I knew it well. Two shots in rapid succession. And then silence. That's what didn't make sense. Screams usually followed gunfire. I palmed my gun and slipped back inside. The hallway was clear. The dressing room remained undisturbed. I pressed my back against the wall and slowly opened the door.

Nothing had changed. But I knew I heard shots, and they had come from somewhere inside this warehouse. My gaze swept the interior. The two guards remained at the front, but the two Axel had seen guarding the side were gone.

I stuck to the walls and moved through the warehouse. The hazy air and poor lighting helped conceal my approach. The men were oblivious. The few who were even aware of the women in the room had other things on their minds besides me. However, the two men with automatic weapons probably wouldn't take kindly to my presence, so I tried to blend in and stay hidden.

What are you doing, Liv? the voice in my head asked. I should be outside waiting for backup. ESU should be sweeping the place, not me. I didn't even have a vest. Still, I couldn't shake the surreal feeling. No one was panicked. No one was hurt. And no one else seemed to have heard the two gunshots. Even the big guns at the door acted nonchalant. Maybe I was wrong.

I hid behind the velvet curtain near the side door. It was cracked open, but Axel had been wrong. It didn't lead outside; it led to a control room. From my position, I could see a dozen monitors and a control board for the sound system and lights. A man sat in a chair, his focus entirely on the screens.

I crept inside, sweeping my aim from side to side, but no one else was in the room. Slowly, I approached the man. One of the screens caught my attention, and I pressed the muzzle of my gun into the back of his head.

"Police," I announced. "Raise your hands slowly, or I'll blow your fucking head off."

He did as I said, and I expertly clicked my handcuff around his right wrist before twisting his arm around the back of the chair. I took a step back, my gun never wavering as I wrestled his other hand behind the back of the chair. Then I shoved my gun into my waistband and bound his hands together.

Tugging his chair away from the control board, I spun him around to face me. "Where are they?" I gestured at the monitor. The bottom screen showed six women trapped in cages.

He chuckled, so I hit him across the face with the butt of my gun. His cheek bled, and he spit. "Fuck you."

"Wrong answer." I reached into his pocket and pulled out his wallet, but just like every other asshole we'd encountered in the course of the investigation, he didn't have an ID. "Tell me where they are." I cocked my gun.

"You're a cop. You can't shoot an unarmed man."

"Wanna bet?"

Briefly, his eyes darted to the screens, and he started jabbering nonsense, asking dozens of questions. He wanted to distract me. He didn't want me to see something. I turned around just in time to see an armed man drag one of the women out by the legs, leaving a bright red smear in her wake.

She'd been shot. Those were the two shots I heard. The cages had to be in this building. But where?

The asshole kept dithering on even more frantically as I clicked keys, toggling the footage and trying to decipher the camera's location. The wheels on his chair made a skidding noise. I turned, and he stopped fidgeting.

"Get up." I grabbed him by the crook of the arm and jerked him out of the chair, knocking it to the floor in my haste. "You're going to take me to them. If anyone shoots at me, the bullet's going through you first."

"I'm not taking you anywhere."

"Then I'll kill you now." I pointed at the screen. "She's either dead or dying. No one gives a shit what a decorated detective does to some asshole killer. We're in a dark warehouse filled with civilians and at least four heavily armed men. I'm just one woman. Who do you think a jury will believe?"

"Fine. There's a hallway just to the right of this room. It leads to the cages."

I found a roll of duct tape on the desk and covered his mouth. I couldn't afford for him to call for help. Since I was alone, I needed the element of surprise, and I couldn't be certain this wasn't a trap. I shoved him out the door and moved to the right. As he said, there was an opening for a hallway a few feet away, concealed by the curtain.

I kept a hand on his shoulder, letting him lead the way down the hall. This wasn't procedure, but nothing about this case had been. I strained to hear sirens, but I didn't hear anything. Was help on the way?

He stopped suddenly, hunching over and jerking away. He tried to knock me into the wall with his shoulder, and I kicked him hard in the stomach. The way he moved triggered a memory of Clarissa Berens' abduction footage. I knew this guy looked familiar. He kidnapped Clarissa.

He barreled toward me again, hoping to push past and escape. He almost succeeded, but at the last second, I grabbed the back of his shirt and swept my leg out. He lost his footing, tripped, and crashed against the wall. He didn't move again. I checked his pulse to find he was out cold. I didn't know how long that would last, but I had to neutralize the armed men. If not, I didn't know if any of the women would survive. I was right; Clarissa was here.

Taking a breath, I slipped through the open doorway. The only sound came from the buzzing of the light fixtures. The cages were pressed against the walls of the room. Unlike the hidden room we found inside the house, the women weren't chained to anything. Instead, they were held prisoner in tiny crates that would have been too cruel to house the K-9 unit.

The wet smear on the floor turned my stomach. The men were close. I could feel it. Shifting my aim from the left to the right, I didn't spot either of the two men. Maybe Axel was wrong. Or maybe it was one gunman, and the other guy was the prick I knocked out.

The nearest woman looked up, and I recognized her from the photos on our board. "Shh," I whispered, "it's okay, Abigail. I'm Detective DeMarco. I'm going to get you out of here."

"How? How do you know my name? How did you know I was here?" Her questions drew the attention of the four other women, who all pleaded with me to let them out.

I looked at their faces, recognizing Clarissa and Yasmine from their photographs. The other two I didn't know. "We've been searching for you. All of you." I examined the cages, unable to figure out the locking mechanism. "I'm going to get you home." I glanced behind me. "Where'd he go?"

"He took Lyla," one of the other women said. "She wouldn't listen. He wanted her to behave, and she just...she said no. He shot her twice."

"All right." The last thing I wanted to do was leave them trapped in this hellhole, but I didn't know how to get them out. I tugged on the cage door, but it didn't budge.

"It's electronic," Clarissa said. "He was bitching that his friend was dicking around instead of paying attention and opening the doors."

"Okay." The unlock mechanism might be in the control room. "I'll be right back."

"You can't leave us," Yasmine said, her voice shaky and desperate. "He might come back. He said he'll kill us if we don't behave. Please don't leave us here."

"Backup should be here any second. I'll be back soon. You're going to be okay." Listening to the desperate cries nearly broke my heart, but I had to find Lyla. I had to stop the animal who took her before he could inflict more damage.

Swallowing, I followed the blood trail away from the cages. It led into an adjoining room, which might have been a storage closet at one point. The only light came from the open doorway, and I reached into my bag for a flashlight before stepping inside. With the flashlight held in my left just beneath my gun, I entered the room. Shelves lined the walls. Near the back wall, I found Lyla.

I swept the beam of light to the left and right, but I didn't see the man. How could he have vanished into thin air? Lyla let out a pained gasp, and I stepped closer, the beam of light darting back and forth. Where was he? After a final check, I crouched down beside her. She'd been shot in the chest, a through and through.

"Lyla?" I asked softly, my voice low. "Where is he?"

Her eyes fluttered. She spoke, but I couldn't hear her. I leaned in closer, and that's when he jumped down from the top of the shelves. Before I could even turn, he wrestled me onto my stomach, locking the crook of his elbow tightly around my neck. I tried to tuck my chin in like we were taught, but he didn't give me enough room. He yanked my hair, holding my head back and in place. In those ten seconds, every mistake and missed opportunity ran through my mind, and then there was nothing.

TWENTY-NINE

A shock of pain erupted across my cheek, but it wasn't enough to force me to open my eyes. "Wake up." He hit me again.

Slowly, I blinked. Where was I? I tried to move but realized two men were holding me down. My head hung off the foot of the bed, and everything was upside down. It was hard to stay focused, and it seemed like any minute I might be sick. "Where am I?"

I tried to lift my head to see the asshole who struck me, but strong hands pushed even harder against my clavicle. I tried to move my legs, but the two men sat on top of my thighs. I turned my head to the side. I didn't see Lyla. If we were still in the converted warehouse, this was a room I hadn't seen before.

Twisting again, I caught a glimpse of one of the men – Oleg Vorshkovich. The other man, the one who had spoken, wore a Guy Fawkes mask over his face. "Were they out of ski masks at Criminals Anonymous?" I asked. "Although I much prefer that getup to homicidal clown." I found my right hand wasn't pinned down and ran my palm over the threadbare spread. "Oh, wait, that would have been too on the nose."

He snorted. It was an ugly, vulgar sound. "You think you're clever?"

"I found you, didn't I?" I swallowed the bile that burned the back of my throat. "We can exchange snippy comments all day, but I have places to be."

"You're not going anywhere until you tell me what the police know." He dismissed Oleg and climbed on top of me, both knees digging into my thighs while his hands held down my shoulders. Oleg disappeared from view only to return with a bucket and a towel. "You decide how painful this will be, Detective DeMarco."

"Too bad I like pain."

He slapped me again, hard enough that I tasted blood. "So do I."

Oleg put the bucket beneath my head and switched places with the Guy Fawkes impersonator. The man in the mask wore a three-piece suit. He took off his jacket, and I caught a glimpse of the designer label. He rolled up his sleeves, and I eyed the flashy timepiece on his wrist.

"Guy Fawkes. That's rather apropos," I said. "The real Fawkes and his Gunpowder Plot failed, and now his effigy gets burned on top of bonfires. So I'm going to make sure you burn for this."

He leaned closer, and the look in his eyes scared the crap out of me. "How much do the police know about my operation?"

"Your operation?" I laughed. "Everyone knows you want to blow up the House of Parliament. That's why you've been stockpiling powder kegs."

"Enough." He nodded to Oleg, who held the towel

firmly against my face.

I couldn't see what was happening, but there was only one way this could go. Within moments, the towel became heavy and suffocating as it took on the water. I held my breath. Struggling would make it worse. I'd drown faster. But he expected my trick and hit me hard enough in the gut to force the air from my lungs. And then I was choking, gasping down water as I struggled for air. When I didn't think I could take it anymore, the water stopped, and he pulled the towel away. I coughed up a lungful of water. My hair soaked, my throat and lungs burning.

"What do they know?" he asked.

"Everything."

"Bullshit."

He shoved the towel over my face again and poured. I sputtered, desperate to breathe. He was still talking, but his words were garbled. My lungs burned from lack of air, and the fear of drowning overtook my senses. Seconds before my body could betray my resolve not to breathe in even more water, he pulled the towel away. Water dripped from my face and hair. After a coughing fit, I gasped for breath.

"I'll ask you one more time. How did you know to come here?"

"We have Dmitri. He told us plenty."

"Dmitri's dead. I made sure of that."

I blinked the water from my eyes. "You killed him?" I remembered the lab coat we found in the motel room. "You infiltrated his hospital room."

Despite the smiling mask, I knew this sicko was smiling underneath too. "I just had to wait for you to leave before I could do it. I didn't want you to recognize me."

That meant I must know who this guy was. Who did I know that Agent Peters didn't? Unless it was

Agent Peters.

"What did the girls at the motel tell you?" the masked man asked.

"Why? So you can kill them too?"

He reached for another giant jug of water. "Do you know who I am?"

I forced myself to laugh. "You're scared. And you should be. Did you honestly believe the moniker Mr. X and a pathetic theater mask were enough to save you?"

This next round of torture lasted even longer. Somewhere between the water and lack of air, I lost consciousness. When I finally came back around, Oleg was pumping his palms up and down on my chest, and the water I coughed up felt too warm, like it had been trapped inside so long it had reached a balmy 98.6 degrees.

"You shut down the motel. You made arrests. Who are the police coming after next?" he asked.

"You."

He reached for the towel.

"Don't," I begged between gasps. My entire body was wracked with shivers, and my head pounded a rhythm in time to my racing pulse. The water in the bucket beneath me was tinged red, and I didn't want to think too hard about why that was.

"Then tell me what I want to know," he shrieked. "How did you find the house and warehouse? How did you know where to look?"

"I told you." I struggled to sit up, but Oleg put his hands against my shoulders and shoved me back against the bed. The wooden frame dug into my shoulder blades. "We have an informant. He told us where to find the car and how to find Clarissa, Lyla, and Abigail." My thoughts went to the locked cages. What happened to them? Were they dead now? "We have the women. We know you're selling them overseas. Interpol has a file on you, on your associates." I smiled, despite my chattering teeth. "You're fucked. It'd be best if you turn yourself in now." I looked again at his jacket, watch, and mask. I'd seen them before.

"Stop wasting my time." He reached for the towel, but I kept talking, hoping my words would hold him off.

"Why'd you do it? Aren't you supposed to stand for female empowerment? Isn't that one of your mission statements? I'm sure I read that in a brochure or on your company website. Maybe it was hanging on the plaque behind your desk."

His anger grew. "Silence."

I couldn't reason with the guy behind the mask, but maybe I could appeal to the Eastern European. "Oleg Vorshkovich," I gasped out. "See, we know everything. And I know he'll kill you next or sell you out to the authorities like he's done to all the others. Like Dmitri and Keith."

Oleg cocked his head up. His grip loosened slightly. "What does Interpol know?"

I used that opportunity to slide down the bed, so my head wasn't hanging quite so far off the edge. Oleg allowed me to move, wanting to look into my eyes while I answered his question. "They have a file on you, Mr. Vorshkovich. They know what you've done, who you work for in Russia. They've been tracking your activities for quite some time. They want your boss. They'll take this prick instead. I can cut you a deal."

While he was distracted by my words, my fingers brushed against the edge of his pants. I coughed again, my entire body jerking against him. It was a trick pickpockets used, and while I'd never snatched a guy's wallet off the street, I managed to snag the switchblade from Oleg's pocket without him noticing. I concealed it beneath my palm, waiting for an opportunity.

"Enough of this. She'll say anything. She wants to scare us. End her." Guy Fawkes moved away from the bed, rolled his sleeves down, and slipped his jacket on. "And clean up when you're finished."

"Wait." I tried to swallow, my throat raw and painful. "How'd you get the FBI badges and access codes?"

The masked man laughed. "I thought you knew everything. I guess you don't, and you never will." He turned to Oleg. "She's yours. You can play with her if you like, but make sure none of this traces back to me. Understand?"

Oleg nodded. The fact that it would all be over soon wasn't comforting. It was morbid.

"Last chance, Oleg," I said. "Everyone knows the truth. You're wanted. Your best bet is to run far and fast. It's the only way of getting out of here. You can't trust him. He kills his own people or convinces them to off themselves, like Keith. Who is he going to send to steal your body from the morgue?" And suddenly, it made sense. "That's why you stole the van from the FBI. He told you to. He knew we'd discover the bodies were gone. He wanted us to find you. He set you up to be his fall guy. That's why he's leaving you behind with me. He'll probably tip the police as soon as he walks out that door."

"That's not true," Guy Fawkes said.

Oleg glared at him and said something in Russian. But the masked man promised to take care of it and headed toward the door. Oleg tugged on my arms, pulling me fully onto the mattress. My shoulder blades scraped painfully against the frame. I hissed, but the sound was cut off when he shoved a pillow against my face. He pressed down hard, holding it tight. At least it was fractionally better than drowning.

With whatever energy I had left, I thrashed and struggled. My limbs brushed against his. Through the pillow, I heard the distinctive sound of a door slamming. Mustering all my strength, I flicked the release and plunged the blade into Oleg's thigh. He howled. The pillow no longer pressed against my face, and I twisted the knife, digging it in deeper. He reared back, blood pumping out of the gaping wound. He pulled the knife free, a shriek erupting from his lips as blood droplets splattered over me, the walls, and the floor. He lunged forward, planning to slice my throat. I rolled off the bed and crashed to the floor just as the blade swung down, slashing into the mattress.

The outer walls shook, and I heard repeated commands echoing. There was a good chance I was hallucinating because the yelling and threats sounded like they were coming from Brad.

"Where is she? What have you done to her?" The walls shook again. "Tell me now." Another two voices joined Brad's, and suddenly, the door burst inward. And Oleg, with the knife in the air, was hit twice with beanbag rounds.

Thunderous footsteps entered the room. "Suspect down." I remained on the floor while two members of ESU cleared the room. "Officer down. Repeat officer down."

Fennel brought up the rear, homing in on me immediately. "Liv." He crouched on the floor, taking in the remnants of the waterboarding. "We need help over here."

I shivered and coughed, weak, dizzy, and spattered in Oleg's blood. "I'm okay." ESU cuffed Oleg, but they were more concerned with my health. "He'll bleed out in under five minutes if you don't get him to a hospital. We might still need him. Get him medical attention. I'm fine."

They looked to Brad, who asked, "You really want to save the asshole who did this to you?"

"Oleg didn't do this." I saw the confusion in Brad's eyes. "He's wearing a three-piece suit and a Guy Fawkes mask. Did you get him?"

"Who?"

"The asshole in the Guy Fawkes mask." I saw the confusion on Brad's face. "*V for Vendetta*."

Brad shook his head. "Maybe he took it off. We found another guy in the hallway." Brad described him, but I was certain it was the asshole I cuffed from the control room.

"Wrong guy. You have to get him before he escapes."

"He won't escape. The building's surrounded. I'm not leaving you, Liv."

"Fennel, if you don't stop him, he'll find a way out and start over somewhere else. I can't live knowing I'm the reason for that. You have to stop him." My eyes met Brad's. I'd never seen him look so scared. I tried to sit up, but I was too shaky. "I'm not going anywhere. You have to nail Dale Crenshaw. Do it for me."

THIRTY

Crenshaw slipped out of the makeshift bedroom. He designed the room in case any of his clients wanted to sample the girls before buying, but that never happened since he needed the privacy to question the detective. She must have been lying, he convinced himself. She never used his name. The things she said were merely speculation. She wanted to scare him, but he wouldn't scare this easily. He had a plan. And he intended to stick with it. But then he heard the echoing words. "Police. Freeze."

"Shit." He darted down a hidden corridor that lined the back of the warehouse. The back hallways and offices were like a maze. He had to get to the side door before they found him.

Pulling the mask off his face, he wasn't sure what to do with it. He couldn't risk leaving it behind. The police would trace it back to him, and his life would be ruined. But it would be game over if they caught him with the mask.

The commands grew louder. He heard gunshots. Oleg must have been eliminated. The detective was right about one thing; he intended to let the Russian take the fall for everything. The teams he hired, the mercenaries at the door, they were all Eastern Europeans and known associates of the Russian.

He entered one of the back offices and stood on a chair to reach the vent. Removing the grate, he stuffed the mask inside and replaced the metal panel. The police would never find it in there. Maybe he'd come back for it later, but right now, he had to get out.

He ran down the hallway to the side door and slipped the key into the lock. Cautiously, he opened the door a crack. Police vehicles were just feet away. He shut the door. He couldn't go out that way. "Fuck."

Crenshaw thought about the costumes in the dressing room. He had those brought here to appease his kinkier clients, but he didn't remember if there were any police jackets in the mix. He had a few from the uniform catalog shoot, but he didn't remember if they were here. He used the warehouse to store a lot of props since he never knew what he'd need or what his buyers might want to see the girls dressed as. Maybe he could get out by pretending to be a cop.

Before he could make it another step, he heard the voice behind him. "Freeze."

Crenshaw raised his hands in the air and slowly turned around. "Thank god." He smiled at the cop. "They lured me here. I've been searching for a way out. The men at the doors have guns. They wouldn't let us leave."

Detective Fennel didn't lower his weapon. "Get down on your knees. Hands behind your head."

Crenshaw slowly knelt on the ground. "You're making a big mistake. I'm not one of them."

"The hell you aren't." Fennel took a step closer. "What's your name?"

Crenshaw sensed this was a trap.

"Answer me."

"I'm innocent. I'm not with them," Crenshaw insisted. "I tried to call for help, but my phone won't work."

"We found the jammer. We found Denis Hiver. And your pal, Oleg Vorshkovich, is on his way to the hospital. Now answer my fucking question."

The blood drained from Crenshaw's face. He knew he was caught. "My name's Stan. Stan Haversham. My ID is in my breast pocket."

Fennel didn't believe him, but he had to make sure. "Reach into your pocket slowly and toss me your ID."

Crenshaw did as he was told, and when Brad reached down to scoop up the wallet, Crenshaw pulled a gun.

* * *

"Gun," I yelled, pushing away from the ESU officer who was helping me down the hallway. My legs wobbled, and I grabbed the wall for support.

My partner didn't need me to make the announcement. He had never taken his eyes off Crenshaw, and when the suspect pulled the gun, Brad fired, hitting Crenshaw squarely in the shoulder. Crenshaw fell backward. The gun clattered to the ground, and Brad jumped on him. Within moments, Crenshaw was on his belly, his hands cuffed behind him.

"You fuck with my partner, and I'll fuck with you." Brad kicked Crenshaw hard in the ribs, and a member of the tactical team pulled him away.

Another officer took over, and they held Brad until he calmed down. When they let go of my partner, Brad stepped away. He picked up the gun Crenshaw had dropped and looked at it. He tucked it into his waistband and retrieved the dropped wallet. *Dale*

Crenshaw.

"I found your gun, Liv." Brad slipped beneath my arm before my legs gave out. "You really need to learn to hang on to this. The city entrusted it to you for a reason."

"Yeah, yeah." I wrapped my arms around his shoulders, and he scooped me off the ground. "Are you okay?"

"I am now."

"What about the women in the cages? And Lyla James? We have to help them."

"Half the force is here. They'll take care of that. Right now, let's just take care of you." He carried me out of the warehouse and into the back of a waiting ambulance.

THIRTY-ONE

When I entered the bullpen the next day, there was a round of applause. Brad, who'd been behind me on the stairs, took some dramatic bows while I rolled my eyes and made my way to my desk. We had a big day ahead of us. We didn't have time for this.

"Good job, DeMarco," Officer Roberts said.

I looked up. That might have been the first nice thing he ever said to me. And it would probably be the last. I nodded and scanned the notes that had piled up on my desk.

Fennel didn't bother to sit down. "Warrant's ready." He eyed me curiously, seeing the dark bruises poking out from under my collar. "You went through something yesterday. Are you sure you don't want to sit this one out?"

"Come on, Brad. This is the fun part. Plus, I want to see this through."

He grabbed some scissors off his desk. "In that case, give me your wrist. I can't spend the day running around with an escaped mental patient."

"They didn't put me in the psych ward," I protested as he cut the hospital bracelet off.

"Clearly, an oversight." He tossed it into the wastebasket.

I finished reading the updates and went into Grayson's office to collect my newly returned service piece. Officers found my cuffs on Denis Hiver, Clarissa's kidnapper. The five women in the cages were in the hospital, undergoing evaluation, but physically, they'd be okay. I hadn't heard what happened to Lyla, and I was afraid to ask.

On my way out, I looked at the board. We never found Tanya, one of the first abductees we knew about. But we found two others we didn't know were missing. I hated to think how many more were out there, who'd already been killed, sold, or worse. Setting my jaw, I followed Fennel to the car. It was time we got answers.

"Hey, talk to me," Brad said. "How'd you know it was Crenshaw? If you hadn't told me it was him, he might have managed to sneak out. Did you see his face?"

"No, but I recognized the suit he wore and his watch. At first, I couldn't be sure, but one of the biggest perks for working at Rogers and Stein is getting to keep the samples advertisers leave behind after shoots. And they had the campaign images plastered on the walls for that designer and that watch. But what gave him away was the mask. The theater company had a room full of donations made by Rogers and Stein. They had a dozen or more of those masks lining the backstage area in the theater. And let's not forget, Crenshaw had access to everyone and everything. He got the fake FBI badges when they shot the photos for the uniform catalog."

Fennel pulled to a stop in front of Crenshaw's

mansion. Dale Crenshaw was in custody. His prints were all over the jugs of water he'd poured down my throat, but we wanted evidence of his other bad acts. "All right. Let's see what we find."

Another team simultaneously served a second search warrant at the modeling agency, but I didn't believe Crenshaw would leave sensitive and damning materials at work, especially when I knew he'd been out sick the last two days. He knew we were coming. He booked two first-class airline tickets to a non-extradition country. Once he dumped the rest of the cargo, he planned to run. If I hadn't found him last night, he'd be on a tropical island sipping mai-tais instead of getting to know his fellow offenders in lockup.

"Mrs. Crenshaw," Fennel said when the suspect's wife opened the door, "we have a warrant to search the property."

Her eyebrows knit together. "Where's my husband? Where's Dale?"

"Ma'am," I nodded to the officers, and they pushed their way inside, "let's go inside and talk."

Mrs. Crenshaw refused to believe any of what we had to say. As far as she was concerned, her husband was a decent and kind man. She insisted he was innocent. But a thorough examination of his office, phone, and computer records proved otherwise. We found offshore numbered accounts. His desk drawer contained documents indicating he owned and registered the dummy corporations and LLCs that rented the motel rooms, the house, and the warehouse. His records went back nearly a decade.

"How many women do you think he's trafficked?" Fennel asked.

I looked at the details on Crenshaw's hidden accounts. "More than we know about. At least we have enough to put him away for consecutive life sentences. Too bad that won't bring any of the women back."

"Maybe we can convince him to cooperate. We can offer him a nice window in his prison cell or maybe a sturdy support beam he can use to hang himself."

"Yeah, maybe." But I doubted he'd talk.

On the drive back to the precinct, my phone rang. "DeMarco, you told me to call if no one came back for that car," Officer Chen said. He'd been sitting on the Monthly Stay Condos since we shut them down. "It's the only one left. I ran the plates. It's registered to a Nathan Lence. According to motel records, he's a guest. But we checked his room. It's completely empty."

"Do you have his photo ID?" I asked. That was the same car Brad and I checked out.

"I'll send it to you now."

I waited for the image to appear, and then I cursed. Immediately, I called to get another warrant. "Change of plans," I said to Brad.

"What's going on?"

"I know who Keith Richardson is." Although the photo ID of Nathan Lence barely resembled the man I encountered on the roof, I remembered his eyes. I'd never forget them. Nathan Lence had a thick, unruly beard, a shaved head, and thick glasses. It was no wonder facial rec had problems identifying him from the photos we had of Keith Richardson. They hardly looked alike.

By the time we made it to Lence's address, a patrol car was waiting outside. I got out of the car and spoke to the officers. The apartment was rented to Nathan Lence and Scarlet Archer, the mother of Lence's only son. According to the birth certificate, Nathan Jr. was three years old.

The warrant hadn't come through yet, but I

knocked on the door anyway. An attractive woman around my age answered. She looked exhausted. Her clothes had food stains, and her hair was messy.

"Ma'am, I'm Detective DeMarco. This is my partner, Detective Fennel."

"Where's Keith?" she asked.

"Keith?" I didn't expect her to use his alias.

"My boyfriend, Nathan." She shook her head. "He goes by Keith. He's been missing. Well, no. That's not true. He left us. He called one night last week and told me he wasn't coming back. He said it was for the best. That he was doing it for our son."

"Your son?" Brad asked, gazing into the apartment.

She realized she should invite us in and stepped away from the door. "He's sick. Really sick. Keith said he'd take care of it. That he'd find a new job. Something that pays well. And we finally caught up on the bills. Nate just went into remission." She dabbed her eyes. "We don't know if it'll last. I don't know why he'd leave now. The hard part's over. Nate needs his dad." She saw the expression on my face, and hers contorted into a silent scream. Brad grabbed her before she collapsed. He helped her to the couch and held out his phone. "Ma'am, do you recognize this man?"

She nodded, her lips trembling. "That's Keith. Where is he?"

"I'm sorry to tell you this." Brad continued as she sobbed.

I turned away. Now I understood what made Keith kill himself. Crenshaw threatened his son and his family. Crenshaw must have paid the boy's medical bills in exchange for Keith finding women to abduct. Suddenly, I didn't feel so good, but I held it together, relieved Fennel was willing to pick up the slack. We didn't need the warrant. Scarlet gave us everything we needed and more. By the time we left, I wanted to try out my own waterboarding techniques on Crenshaw.

"He's not innocent," Fennel said. "Keith chose to take those women. Not only did he abduct them, but he killed Ingrid. Sure, he needed the money, but there are other ways. Ways that don't destroy lives and families. He inflicted more hurt on this world than what he faced." Fennel forced me to look at him. "It's not your fault that little boy doesn't have a dad and that woman doesn't have her partner. Keith put himself in this position. He could have come to us at any time, but he didn't. His death is his own."

"I know. It just sucks."

"I thought you said this was the fun part."

"I was wrong."

We spent the rest of the day processing evidence, speaking to witnesses and the men we had in custody, and building our case. Agent Peters came in to assist. Dale Crenshaw would be facing both state and federal charges in addition to his international crimes. His position at Rogers and Stein had allowed him to meet many famous people. Some of those people had security details made up of former federal agents. We suspected that's how he found out how to gain access to the FBI's motor pool and the ME's office. The FBI was looking into possible security breaches and would bring anyone who posed a threat to security in for questioning.

At least Crenshaw would never be able to hurt anyone again. Hopefully, Interpol would be able to use our evidence to shut down the overseas branches of the human trafficking ring. They already had the Russian in custody. Based on Crenshaw's records, he bought and sold to South America and Eastern Europe. This was so much bigger than the four missing women. This was monumental.

The FBI picked up Ivan Sergei at the airport. After the raid, he tried to flee. But his passport was flagged, and he was arrested. Oleg Vorshkovich survived, and that gave us two accomplices who'd be more than happy to flip on Crenshaw and their Russian boss in exchange for asylum and protection.

Initially, Crenshaw used his position at Rogers and Stein to find women. He approached those who weren't selected by the modeling agency and offered them alternative gigs. That's how Shana and the others ended up in the motel. He didn't know if there was a market for women with their particular attributes, so he'd hold on to them for six months at a time. If one of his buyers selected one from the stable, he'd tell her he had a job for her – that it was her big break. She'd be flown out of the country and sold into slavery. And if not, he'd send her on her way. The women lucky enough not to be chosen were unharmed and released, clueless to the potential danger they had faced. But sometimes, Crenshaw's buyers wanted women with different attributes, and that led Crenshaw to enlist Keith's help.

Since Crenshaw knew Keith from his work at the community center, collecting donations from Rogers and Stein, he must have known of Keith's financial predicament. So he turned Keith into an asset. Unfortunately, Keith wasn't a criminal mastermind. The police eventually realized the women he abducted were missing, so when Ingrid, our Jane Doe from the alley, had overheard the men talking in the motel room, she realized this wasn't her chance at modeling stardom and escaped.

She sought help but didn't get very far before Ivan realized she was gone and recaptured her. Ivan called Crenshaw, and Crenshaw told Keith to take care of it. That's when everything started falling apart.

Desperate, Crenshaw planned to set up his buyers to take the fall, but we intervened just in time.

"Any idea where Tanya or the others have disappeared over the years?" I asked Agent Peters when he left the interrogation room.

"Interpol agents are raiding compounds as we speak. Hopefully, Crenshaw's buyers have easily traceable records. I'm keeping my fingers crossed that we find them."

"Me too."

Peters clapped me on the shoulder, and I tried to hide my wince. "For a moment, back at the hospital, I got the distinct impression you thought I might be behind this."

"Well, Crenshaw orchestrated Dmitri's death. And he had Oleg and Dmitri steal the van from the FBI. I was just following the evidence."

"Next time, give your friends with badges the benefit of the doubt. Most of the time, we're the good guys."

"Well, Oleg and Dmitri also had badges. You can see why I was confused."

Peters smiled. "You're forgiven, Detective. And thanks for bringing this to our attention."

I leaned back in my chair and closed my eyes. We just had to put on the final touches, but the case was closed. Maybe I'd take a few personal days to regroup and recover. Fennel finished his interview with David Hennen and returned to his desk.

"Looks like Hennen's clean. He told us he let Keith drive the van, and we found prints inside the back that are a match. Keith must have used the community center's van to abduct Lyla."

"How is she?" I asked.

"Lucky. The bullets didn't hit any vital organs. She'll be fine."

"That's good to hear." I narrowed my eyes. "I'm confused about something."

"What's that?"

"How'd you know where I was?"

"Kincaid called and tipped us off. I also have a feeling he's the reason the warehouse was empty when we got there. Those businessmen you kept talking about, not a single one was in the main room. Neither were the escorts or caterers."

"You think he cleared the place?"

"Weren't those his clients or associates?" Fennel asked.

I shrugged. "Do you want to bring him in?"

"He saved you. And when we did a deep dive into his financials on the last case, nothing indicated he's involved with human trafficking or Dale Crenshaw. As far as I'm concerned, this is his one free pass. But it's up to you."

I stared at the heaping pile of paperwork. "I don't want to fill out any more forms, so we'll let this slide for now. Officers followed up with him, right?"

Brad nodded.

"Okay. Then I'll just finish this and go home. I could use a break."

"You deserve it."

"We deserve it," I corrected, but the dark cloud remained over Fennel's head.

THIRTY-TWO

Before going home that night, I stopped by Spark. Rick nodded at me when I walked up to the door. "Good evening, Liv. The boss is expecting you."

"Expecting me?" I wasn't even sure I'd stop by.

"Mr. Kincaid's waiting in his office. Drinks are on the house." He opened the door.

"Thanks, Rick."

I stepped inside, expecting the usual dim lights, loud music, and women dancing in cages. Instead, a piano sat in the middle of the dance floor, and a singer was hired to entertain for the evening. It was a somber night for thrill-seekers.

I took a familiar path past the bar and down the private hallway. I knocked on Axel Kincaid's open door. "Rick said you're expecting me."

Axel looked up. "Something told me you might stop by. Are you here to ask for your waitress job back, or are you here to arrest me?" He held up his wrists. "You can cuff me, but you should pat me down first. Who knows what I might be concealing?"

Taking a seat in front of his desk, I glanced down at the files and papers spread across the mahogany surface. "What's this?"

"If you must know, I'm reevaluating Spark's membership. In the last twenty-four hours, I've drastically reduced my clientele. Perhaps you noticed the lull."

"I need names."

He smirked. "Do you have a warrant?"

"I could get one."

"It'd be a waste of time. Unfortunate shredding accident. See?" He held up his pinky. "Papercut." He got up from his desk and reached for a bottle of brandy he kept on the cart in the corner. "Are you on duty?"

"No."

"So this is a social visit." He poured two glasses and brought them over. He sat on the edge of the desk and stared down at me while I sipped from the crystal glass. "You can't figure out why I would help you after everything you did to me." He took a sip. "You betrayed my trust, penetrated my club, lied to me, and used every bit of it against me. Honestly, Liv, I don't know why I helped you either. You don't deserve my help."

"I was just doing my job, Mr. Kincaid."

He took another swallow, hiding the bitterness. "I told you we're not that different. I run this place to keep people from going crazy and doing insane shit out there. I give them an outlet, but that doesn't mean I condone disgusting and depraved acts. Human trafficking, sex slaves, that isn't on the menu at Spark. It shouldn't be on the menu anywhere. I just did what any good citizen would do."

"So why'd you clear the warehouse before the cops arrived? Why won't you give me the names of the men who are interested in buying sex slaves? They'll just find another source. You can't stop them, Axel, but I can."

Kincaid's blue eyes flashed to me. "It's been handled."

"What does that mean?"

"It's probably best if you don't concern yourself with those details." He put the glass down and grasped my chin. Gently, he touched his thumb to my split lip. "You shouldn't have gone back inside. They could have killed you. From the rumors I heard, they came close."

"I didn't have a choice. That's the job."

"You should get a new one."

"You sound like my mother." I pulled away from him and drained the glass. "Assuming nothing pops up, I'm willing to let this one slide. Let's call it even." I put the glass down on the desk and stood.

"We're not even, Liv." He ran his fingers along my wrist. "This makes you oh for two. You owe me. And next time, I'm cashing in."

"I didn't realize you needed the money. Come down to the station and fill out the paperwork. You'll get paid like the rest of the department's CIs."

"I wasn't talking about money."

"If you think you can put a cop on the take, I'll arrest you right now."

"I wasn't talking about that either." He ran a thumbnail down my hand, and I stepped away from him. "Your partner just pulled up. Tell him to come inside and have a drink. I insist."

"Fennel's here?"

Axel pointed to the monitor on the wall behind me, and I wondered if Brad had put a tracker on my cell phone. After what happened yesterday, I wouldn't doubt it.

"Thanks for the offer, but we'll have to decline. It could be construed as a bribe."

"You're determined to find some reason to arrest me, aren't you?" Axel asked. "You just can't wait to get me in cuffs again." Ignoring him, I went to the door. "Liv, wait a sec." He put his glass down and approached me. "Regardless of what you believe, I'm not a bad guy. And I'm glad you're okay. Try to stay that way." He kissed my cheek. "Stay safe out there."

Shaking off my confusion, I went outside and met my partner. "What are you doing here?"

"Apparently, we had the same thought." Brad scratched his head and eyed the front of the club. "Did he tell you anything?"

"I thought you said you were letting this go."

Brad gave me a challenging look. "You said the same thing." He chuckled. "Great minds."

"Obviously." I bit my lip and glanced back at Spark. "He won't snitch."

"He did for the DEA."

"Yeah, and I bet they had some serious leverage. We don't." I rubbed my sore shoulders and grimaced. "There's something I need to talk to you about. Come back to Emma's, and I'll grill up those grass-fed steaks and make some sweet potato fries."

"You're hurt. I'll make the steaks."

After dinner, I broke the news to Brad. "Remember when I turned in my transfer papers?"

"That was months ago."

"Yeah, well, Grayson told me after we closed this case, my request would get fast-tracked."

Brad stared down at his napkin. "You wanted out of intelligence. You've never liked the look of impropriety, having your commanding officer be the same man who was your dad's partner." He looked up at me. "Where will you go?"

"I don't know." For some reason, tears started to well. Man, I needed sleep. "I don't want to leave you. You're the best partner a girl could have."

"I'm also the only person willing to put up with your craziness." He pointed to the top of his head. "This morning, I found a gray hair. I pulled it out, but I'm pretty sure you're the one who put it there."

"Brad, I'm serious. I can't just leave you."

"Let me tell you something. You have to do what's best for you. Working these undercover gigs isn't good for you. Hell, it isn't good for me either. I can't even leave you alone for half a second without you doing something absolutely insane. I can't lose you, Liv, but if saving you means we're not partners anymore, then we're not partners anymore."

"Brad, c'mon, you don't mean that."

He pushed away from the table. "No, I guess I don't. But after the way this case resolved, I need to make some changes too. So decide what's best for you. Working undercover will get you killed, Liv, and I won't survive losing you like that. So if you get a better offer, take it." He grabbed his jacket and went to the door.

"Brad," I followed him, feeling as though I'd just been sucker-punched, "I'm sorry."

He turned and smiled. "No reason to be. I always have your back. Just know that." He pressed his lips against my forehead before opening the apartment door. "Enjoy your time off. I'll see you Monday."

THIRTY-THREE

By Monday, everything was back to normal. Fennel acted like we'd never had our conversation. We turned everything over to the DA's office. The prosecutor was confident he had a strong case, and the judge agreed. Crenshaw was denied bail. And the FBI and Interpol continued to dig deeper into the matter. They already conducted several overseas raids and recovered another seven women Crenshaw had trafficked. They even had a strong lead on locating Tanya.

The hospital called to tell us Martha was bouncing back and would be released by the end of the week, and Lyla was already back at home. Grayson called me into his office to tell me the good news.

"You saved them and countless others. Good job." The captain closed the blinds. "Like I told you last week, your transfer request was approved. Homicide's hoping to poach you. They think you have some serious investigative chops they could use. It's a good posting. It isn't intelligence, but it's comparable. They'll keep you busy and on your toes." He slid the paperwork over to me. "It's yours if you want it."

"Captain, I love being here. I love working for you. You've taught me so much."

He waved away my sentiments. "Enough of that, Liv. I promised Vince I'd watch out for you, but things get sticky. We have jobs to do, and keeping that promise and upholding the oath we took gets a little dicey sometimes. You have no idea how many times I've thought about assigning you to a desk just because Vince might think the undercover assignment was too dangerous for his little girl."

I laughed. "So this hasn't been easy for you, either?"

"I didn't become a cop for easy. And neither did you."

"No, sir." I stared out the blinds, but Brad wasn't at his desk. "Fennel's a good cop."

"One of the best. You're our dream team. I hate to lose you."

"I don't want to break what isn't broken."

"It's rare to find a partner like that. You hold on to him as long as you can." Grayson handed me the form, and I went back to my desk.

After sitting on the idea for a few days, I filled out the paperwork and spoke to the homicide lieutenant. Starting next shift, I'd be reporting to him. Grayson knew I was leaving, but I didn't say anything to anyone else. I didn't want to spend a night in a bar recapping cases and listening to embarrassing stories.

"Are you really doing this?" Fennel watched as I packed up my desk. The bullpen was nearly empty at this time of night, which is why I waited. "This is what you want?"

"When I first got assigned to this unit, I wanted to prove myself. To show that I was more than Captain Vince DeMarco's daughter. But after this case, after the things we've seen, I don't have anything left to prove."

"So why are you leaving?" Fennel asked.

"Because of you, and Emma, and my mom."

Fennel licked his lips. "It's because of what that fucking bastard did to you."

"No, but you're right. Undercover's hard. I didn't even go undercover for this case, but it made me realize how much life I'm missing out on every time I get an assignment like that. I don't want to do it this extensively anymore. I want my own place. I want to be me. If I disappear, I want the people I love to notice and not think I'm just working another deep cover assignment. But I'll miss you so much." I rubbed my eyes.

"Hey, nothing's going to change. I'll still be around all the time. You'll see." He jerked his chin toward the door. "Now go home. Get some sleep. You have a big day tomorrow. It's your first day at a new school, and you want to make a good first impression, right?"

"You're such a dork."

"Night, Liv."

"Bye, Brad."

The next morning I reported to homicide. Phones rang. Detectives and officers bustled about. It felt just like intelligence.

I knocked on the lieutenant's door. "Detective DeMarco reporting for duty, sir."

He pointed to a desk in the corner. "That's your spot. The guy at the adjoining desk is your partner. Say hi. Get settled. You have any questions, ask one of the other detectives. There should be a stack of open cases on your desk. You might as well get started."

"Yes, sir." Obviously, this was a sink or swim kind of place.

The man seated at the desk linked to mine wore a

baseball cap. He had his head down, searching the bottom drawer for something. I looked around uncertainly. At least I wasn't the only female detective in the unit. That was something. I put my bag down, removed my nameplate, a few office supplies, and took a seat in my chair.

"Hi, I'm Liv DeMarco," I said. "I believe I'm your new partner."

The man slammed the bottom drawer. "It took you long enough to get here."

"Excuse me?"

"You're late. Didn't anyone ever tell you how important first impressions are?" He slid his nameplate to face me, and I stared at it. *Detective B. Fennel.* I'd been staring at that nameplate every day for the last two years. He took the cap off, and my jaw dropped.

"What the hell are you doing here?"

Brad grinned. "You never listen. I go where you go."

"You can't be here."

"Why not?"

"They never transfer partners. Teams don't get to stay together. You know that."

"So you transferred out of intelligence to get away from me?"

"No." I lowered my voice and glanced around. "No," I repeated.

"Okay, so we're good." He slid a folder closer to me. "I think we should start with this one. It's cold, but it'll give us a chance to dip our toes in the water."

"You don't like bodies." No matter how hard I tried, I couldn't wrap my mind around this. Maybe I was dreaming.

"If they're already dead when I get to them, then I don't have to feel guilty about not saving them. My therapist thinks this might work out better. It will be less of a trigger."

"Okay."

When I continued to stare at him, Brad snapped his fingers in front of my face. He glanced around and leaned closer. "Liv, you're a DeMarco. Even though you're not willing to exploit that fact, I am, and so is Captain Grayson. The department made an exception for us. That last case earned me some major brownie points too, and I'm not complaining. So stop making a spectacle and let's get to work. You're embarrassing me."

"My dad did this."

"Vince called, asked if I had any interest in changing units, and pulled some strings. Apparently, Grayson told him we make a good team and you were going to miss me. Obviously, the commissioner agreed." He grinned. "Don't make me regret this."

"I won't." I smiled. "I promise."

Unforeseen Danger

DON'T MISS DEADLY DEALINGS, THE
NEXT INSTALLMENT IN THE LIV
DEMARCO SERIES.

SIGN UP TO BE NOTIFIED ABOUT NEW
RELEASES AT:

WWW.ALEXISPARKERSERIES.COM/NEWSLETTER

ABOUT THE AUTHOR

G.K. Parks is the author of the Alexis Parker series. The first novel, *Likely Suspects,* tells the story of Alexis' first foray into the private sector.

G.K. Parks received a Bachelor of Arts in Political Science and History. After spending some time in law school, G.K. changed paths and earned a Master of Arts in Criminology/Criminal Justice. Now all that education is being put to use creating a fictional world based upon years of study and research.

You can find additional information on G.K. Parks and the Alexis Parker series by visiting our website at
www.alexisparkerseries.com

Made in the USA
Middletown, DE
21 August 2025